ICE-X '86

Freezing the Cold War

The 1986 Top Secret Mission of the Arctic

The Story Can Now Be Told

L. Joseph Martini

iUniverse, Inc.
Bloomington

ICE-X '86
Freezing the Cold War

iUniverse books may be ordered through booksellers or by contacting:

iUniverse
1663 Liberty Drive
Bloomington, IN 47403
www.iuniverse.com
1-800-Authors (1-800-288-4677)

ISBN: 978-1-4502-9904-6 (sc)
ISBN: 978-1-4502-9905-3 (ebook)

Printed in the United States of America

iUniverse rev. date: 03/09/2011

Dedicated to the scientists and engineers
who work behind the scenes in keeping
world peace.
Their stories of loyal service
and personal sacrifice
are seldom told.

"…*what you do at the top of the world, gentlemen, will influence the course of history.*"

—Secretary of the Navy John F. Lehman Jr., July 1985

"*My v bitvakh reshayem sud'bu pokoleniy. My k slave Otchiznu svoyu povedyom!*"

["In battles we shall decide the fate of generations. We shall lead to the glory of the Motherland!"]

—Captain Leonid Glamouri of the USSR-K240

Acknowledgments

Many people deserve special thanks in the production of this book. Sincere thanks to the people who read the early and final manuscripts for scientific and military accuracy without security compromise. Most of those people cannot be named because of their military and other staff positions. Those whose names can be listed are: Jim Fallin, Public Affairs Officer at the Naval Ocean Systems Center (now Space and Naval Warfare Systems Center Pacific (SSC Pacific), San Diego, CA), and Bob Anderson and his staff at the Naval Office of Information, West Hollywood.

I also extend thanks to Brian McHenry, Casey Robertson, Joshua Romero, and Professor Dean Nelson, Ph.D. (director of journalism at PLNU, San Diego) for their helpful advice and criticism. Special thanks to Ed Spivey Jr. for help with embellishing the descriptive portions of the story. Thanks to Fran Nystrom for her journalist's eye. And I greatly appreciate Carolee Linekin for her detailed proof reading and text correction. Without all of you this book would not exist.

Thanks to the staff of iUniverse Publishing who worked on this book. Your attention to detail and patient professionalism is greatly appreciated. Thanks to Elaine Ward for transforming my ideas into a compelling cover design.

Preface

By the mid-1980s, the massive Soviet naval fleet had grown to almost 400 submarines, 100 of which were the silent and undetectable nuclear missile carriers that posed the greatest strategic threat to the United States. According to Naval Intelligence, nowhere was this threat greater than at the top of the world, where Soviet forces could sail below the Arctic ice to within easy striking distance of the United States.

In 1986, a team of U.S. military and civilian technicians was sent to the North Pole to test a top secret weapons program which, if successful, could for the first time counter the Soviet's fearsome first-strike missile capability. Working in the harsh conditions of the Arctic ice pack—and facing the daunting task of disproving long-held military and scientific beliefs—would the team prove once and for all that submarines cannot hide under the polar cap? Could they prove submarines cannot evade the torpedoes that were America's only undersea tactical defense? Would these tests be successful and culminate President Ronald Reagan's "Peace through Strength" philosophy, the philosophy which historians are saying brought an end to the Cold War?

Now, more than 25 years later, the story can finally be told.

CONTENTS

Acknowledgments ix

Preface xi

1. A Question of Strategic Advantage 1

2. Sub…Mission...9

3. Putting the Team Together................................... 15

4. The Ultimate Game of Warfare...............................27

5. Ice Camp 39

6. Keeping Score 43

7. A Service of Sacrifice.......................................57

8. Nature's Perils 69

9. The Dream 79

10. Torpedo Tests with a Twist...............................89

11. Suspicion to Paranoia 105

Epilogue..119

The Submarines: 121

Official U.S. Photos 125

Movie Trailer: 131

Main Cast of Characters: 137

CHAPTER 1

A Question of Strategic Advantage

April 1986

Three hundred miles south of the North Pole lies the Alpha Cordillera region of the Arctic ice pack. In early spring, the sun is still low in the sky covering the mountainous blue-white ice formations with rainbow colors that give the shadows a spectacular and vibrant beauty. But the five men that braced themselves against a forty-mile-an-hour snowstorm were not interested in natural Arctic beauty, only in steadying a 500-pound object hanging precariously over a large hole in the ice. Gortex hoods and plexiglass goggles obscured the determination in their faces. Their gloved hands moved in practiced coordination as the device was lowered into the freezing water. One of the men pulled back a flap of his parka and looked at his sub-zero watch, then nodded toward his companions. The static sound of a walkie-talkie cut through the wind with a single word.

"Fire!"

Beneath the ice pack there was no hint of the storm above. Light penetrated the watery depths through large cracks in the ice pack which were intermittently freezing and then ripping open again with dynamic pressures of the ocean currents and Arctic winds.

Semi-translucent icicle formations—mammoth stalactites hanging in lengths of 90 feet or more—pointed to the ocean floor, casting undulating shadows onto the steel hull of a submarine as it moved silently along. Ominous in its bulk, like a huge sightless whale, the sub glided past one grouping of stalactite formations. A ribbon of light partially illuminated the inscription on its sail, "666." The sub turned toward another ice formation, then descended, moving beyond view on the other side. Recovering from this intrusion, the cold waters stilled and resumed a state of quiet and dark isolation.

In the distance an object appeared, moving through the water. As it neared, the shape of a torpedo became clear and it continued spiraling down at idle speed in the direction of the diminishing tail of the submarine. Functioning on search mode, the torpedo's electronic seekers sent out audio pulses into the water ahead. As the pulses reached out to the distant sub the return echo triggered an immediate course change by the torpedo. The submarine had become aware, too, as its on-board electronics registered the pulses of the torpedo.

*   *   *

On-board the submarine the sonar operator alerted the captain, "Torpedo in the water! Intermittent pings, Captain. Far off our aft-starboard quadrant.

"Port heading forty-five!" Captain Smith shouted to the helmsman. Then turning to his sonar man, he asked, "Grahams, didn't you say those large ice forms were ahead, to our port quadrant?"

"Yes Sir, coming up at forty degrees now," Grahams quickly replied. "They're large enough to hide behind."

"Perfect! That heading will minimize our profile 'till we get behind their protection. Let's make it happen!" The captain proceeded to give orders to the helmsman as the sonar man revised their location relative to the ice forms.

*   *   *

The submarine sped up and increased its angle towards the ceiling of ice and cover of stalactite projections. A few return pings off its hull gave the torpedo a new heading. It quickened its speed for ninety seconds. But as the submarine slowed and coasted to a stop behind a large ice formation, the torpedo lost ping-return confirmation and slowed its speed. Twenty more seconds and it started a dive, its intent to reach a deeper circle-pattern and look up toward the ice ceiling for the target it had lost.

*   *   *

"Captain, I think we've lost that torpedo, broken trail," Grahams reported with excitement. "But now I'm getting a submarine profile far off and deep. Too large to be one of ours."

In the distant deep coasted the massive hull of a stealth submarine—much larger than the 666-sub. The large, quiet sub was deeper than the diving torpedo, but still within its acquisition range. As the torpedo began to level off and turn into its circular search pattern, it caught a glimpse of the silent submarine. With the confirmation of a few return pings, it quickly interrupted its search pattern. It had acquired a new target.

The torpedo pings were too loud for the crew of the massive, double-hulled submarine not to have noticed. The coasting sub came alive, taking up an aggressive speed and bearing in hopes of evasion. The torpedo ping rate increased against its fleeing target. The race was on.

The torpedo switched from acquisition mode to attack-pinging mode. With a jet of exhaust from its counter rotating prop shafts, it accelerated to impact speed.

The submarine changed course, then changed again to a different bearing, seeking to create an erratic directional signature to confuse the torpedo's sonar. But the torpedo's fins swiveled in reaction, as if choreographed, and guided the undersea missile toward its target. The submarine accelerated to top speed into the dark as the torpedo closed in. A chorus of pings and echoes provided a deathly soundtrack to the inevitable.

*   *   *

Pentagon Meeting

Nine months earlier, on a warm, cloudless July day in Arlington, Virginia, five men stood in the Pentagon office of John Lehman Jr., Secretary of the Navy. Two uniformed Admirals and a Captain talked casually with two men dressed in suits. Lehman walked through the door. He was in a hurry.

"Gentlemen, sorry I'm late. These are hectic times."

Moving quickly to his desk he sat down, folded his hands in front of him and spoke with forcefulness. "I just came from the President's staff meeting where I briefed him on the program. He was delighted. We are going to prove once and for all the technological advancements of our U.S. strategic capabilities and then, to quote the President, we'll 'send a message to the world that the U.S. will always be one step ahead of the Soviets.'"

The five men glanced at each other, maintaining a neutral demeanor. Each one hoped the Secretary was right. And each one had his doubts. Lehman looked from one to another, "I hope you guys introduced yourselves."

Admiral William Gooluc started to reply, but Lehman interrupted, "Of course you all know Admiral James Watkins, Commander of Naval Operations," nodding toward the elderly officer standing at his side. "He's drafting the mission orders we'll transmit to the sub skippers when they reach the Arctic." Admiral Watkins, maintaining his stern composure, simply nodded, his face portraying the gravity of the project.

"Those orders will guarantee a successful outcome of strictly objective torpedo tests against our submarines. No matter what the final outcome, gentlemen, you should know the importance of these tests is immense!" Lehman's words seemed to press down on the composure of the others in the room, except for Admiral Watkins, whose face and gaze did not change. His face reflected the stories of war and the merits of righteous causes; a man whose composure beckoned a look into the future, a future that depended on victories in the present. The ribbons on his chest suggested that his face had earned its silent and stern demeanor.

Lehman continued his introductions, "Admiral Gooluc here is the CO from the Naval Ocean Systems Center. I think you know Captain Clifford Dredge," gesturing to a tall officer with the slight paunch that even his career military bearing couldn't quite hide. "He will be heading up the military aspects of the ice camp, a good fit, since he has sixteen years of experience as a submarine skipper himself."

A "good fit," to say the least, Dredge thought to himself, still smarting from being passed over to be aboard one of the test submarines. A veteran sub skipper, his career was sputtering to an end behind a desk.

The discontent he felt was like a bad taste that he couldn't get out of his mouth. Still, he was the sworn enemy of his nation's enemies, and he wanted to play any role that put the U.S. on the upside against the Soviets. Time to make lemonade, he muttered to himself.

"He'll be invaluable," Lehman assured the group. "Dredge will anticipate what's on the minds of the other sub skippers involved in the tests." Snapped from his dour self-reflection, Dredge displayed a self-confident smile that acknowledged the remark, and stood a bit taller. He was already taller than the others, and was in fact larger than average for a submariner. His broad chest comfortably displayed the ribbons recognizing his years of authority, even though much of those years were spent in a slightly stooped posture. Avoiding painful contact with bulkheads is one of the first lessons a taller submariner learns.

Following up on Lehman's nods toward Dredge's service and expertise, Gooluc added, "Yes, the captain has actually been out at our center a couple of times. I am sure he'll be an asset to the torpedo team." He turned toward one of the men in civilian clothes, "And this is Alex Trinola, Secretary Lehman." A short, muscular man with a neatly trimmed mustache reached a thick hand out to the Secretary, in many ways his physical opposite. The prim, light complexioned Lehman—involuntarily telegraphing his ivy-league education and culture—closed his own hand over Trinola's, the grip confirming each man's confidence in himself. A political appointee's blue eyes stared back at the dark pupils of the journeyman, Trinola.

Gooluc continued, "He's from our San Diego Systems Center and will be heading up the torpedo team. He's got all the expertise necessary to do the job and then some, coming up through the ranks from a navy technician to branch head manager of the torpedo division. He knows everything there is to know about torpedoes, sir." (Even aiming them at our own submarines? the Secretary silently asked himself. We shall see.)

"Pleased to meet you Secretary Lehman," Trinola said, breaking off the handshake. "This project is certainly challenging, but I am sure our team can do it. In fact, I told my wife and kids about how much I was looking forward to meeting you today."

Trinola looked away quickly, instantly regretting his last comment. Sometimes I just say too much, he winced to himself. He hoped the errant comment about telling his wife and kids did not reveal a lack of discretion. Trinola was always quick to speak his mind because of his dominant personality. Working his way up the corporate ladder from the very bottom required no small amount of self-confidence, especially when the bottom was a mere Associates Degree in drafting and design. But he was a fast learner with natural leadership skills. And his relatively low station in life—compared to the multi-degreed colleagues with whom he often shared projects—endeared him to the working stiffs at the center, even when it took more time for his more-educated managers to accept him. Even so they always did. If this Navy program was successful, Trinola would probably make division-head level, and earn all the respect he deserved. Knock on wood, he said to himself.

Lehman turned toward the last man in the room: "Oh, Mr. Trinola, you'll want to meet Mr. Ross Spiry," gesturing toward a middle-aged auburn-haired man in a dark gray suit. Spiry's tie clasp displayed a fifteen year insignia of the TIC (Technical Intelligence Collection), a little-known branch of the even lesser-understood Defense Intelligence Agency.

"He is one of our best Washington analysts and will be assisting your team. He'll be my personal liaison with you, and will be keeping me informed, sending your test data through Capt. Dredge."

Trinola shook Spiry's hand as he searched for eye contact through Spiry's somewhat darkened, automatic shade-changing glasses. Their eyes met for a moment, but Spiry appeared quite shy, nodding his head, and not saying a word.

Lehman looked at his wristwatch.

"Well, gentlemen, it's been nice meeting you all. I guess we're all set, then. These tests will finally prove the capabilities of subs verses torpedoes. Good luck."

"Oh, and there is just one more thing: The schedule has been moved up. The President and I are counting on these tests for spring of '86. That gives you less than nine months to get up there and finish the job."

Trinola and the two admirals looked at each other in amazement, knowing full well what this accelerated schedule would mean. There would be some sleepless nights, especially for the torpedo team, and rest is always mission critical in the field.

Captain Dredge, looking less worried, said, "Our subs will be ready, sir—always ready to show everyone how we can evade torpedoes, even our own torpedoes."

With another quick look at his wristwatch, Lehman concluded, "Gentlemen, if there aren't any questions, I'm afraid I'll have to leave. Wouldn't you know, another meeting."

Capt. Dredge stepped forward raising his hand, "Ah... there is just one thing that I'm not sure of, Secretary Lehman. What is going to prevent Russian involvement in our tests, sir? With the shooting down of that Korean 747 two years ago—ah, even though it breached their air space—the Russians are more trigger-happy than ever."

Lehman stepped from behind his desk as the door was opened from outside the hall by a perfectly-timed aide. "Listen, gentlemen," he said, perturbed and with a slight edge in his voice, "Everything will be taken care of. Just make sure those tests proceed according to schedule. There is no need to be concerned about your precious submarines, Capt. Dredge. The Russians will not get involved."

Admiral Gooluc took two steps toward the Secretary, blocking his view of Dredge and preventing him from commenting further. "Capt. Dredge brings up a legitimate concern, Mr. Secretary. Don't we have to take every contingency into consideration?"

"And one of those contingencies Mr. Secretary," Trinola added, his words overlapping Admiral Gooluc's, "Is that the strategic scenarios of our torpedoes could be compromised, invalidating all our tests."

"Gentlemen, gentlemen." Lehman smiled, taking a step away from his desk. "Don't worry about Soviets. I've taken personal responsibility to ensure that Russian subs will not be present up there. In fact, I am planning to fly up there for the culmination of the tests.

"Now, AGAIN, if you will excuse me gentlemen," Lehman gestured toward the open door.

The men filed out of the room, but Lehman called to Dredge, "Just a minute Capt. Dredge. May I speak to you for a moment?

"Close the door, please."

In the hall, outside the now closed door, Alex Trinola turned toward Admiral Gooluc as they began to walk slowly away from Lehman's office. "Admiral, I appreciate your concern about Russian involvement in our tests—not just because of the effects upon our center, but also how detrimental that could be on the entire program and our U.S.

strategic capabilities. No telling what could happen if the Russians got tangled up with our torpedoes."

Gooluc nodded his head, his pace slowed as he glanced back down the hall. "I think it was good of you and Dredge to confront Secretary Lehman back there, even though he seemed a little annoyed. In these kinds of things you always have to speak your mind. In fact, that's part of why I picked you to lead the team. You don't hold back."

Trinola's face softened as the two men turned the corner, taking a collective backward glance at the door to Lehman's office. They did not speak further, but each wondered if Dredge was getting a dressing down, or if new wrinkles or last-minute plans were being discussed—behind closed doors—between Lehman and Dredge. Gooluc hoped his team would hold together and trust each other with this critical mission. But a private one-on-one conversation, especially behind closed doors, was not a good way to begin.

CHAPTER 2

Sub...Mission

Nine months later, 300 miles south of the North Pole, a submarine quietly cruised in the dark waters 450 feet below the surface. Slowly moving between huge stalactite ice formations, the USS Hawkbill (SSN-666) eased its way toward Canada on a mission as yet unknown. In the commander's quarters, Captain Robert Smith inserted his key into the ship's safe, as Lieutenant Commander Jonathan Maple looked on. Maple rubbed his big hands together, trying to physically focus the combination of emotions he'd been feeling since the ship pushed out of the Maine harbor two weeks ago. Sailing without full orders is not unprecedented, but it was a first for him in the five years he'd been second-in-command, and he suspected the captain was feeling some of the same trepidation. But the captain seldom betrayed his feelings, only his resolve to do his duty. And they were about to find out precisely what that was.

The small safe opened with a surprisingly loud clank, a reminder that it was not only bomb proof but would remain intact---and unopened---even if the ship went down. The U.S. Navy kept its secrets, sometimes forever. Smith reached in and pulled out a crème-colored envelope and laid it on his small desk. Pulling his lamp closer, he signed the printed signature line near the clasp, added date and time, and slid it toward his second-in-command to repeat the ritual. Smith then unwrapped the twine from the clasp, broke the seal, and pulled a single typed page from within. He read the orders silently, then handed the sheet to Maple, who bent his considerable bulk down to hold the page closer to the light.

> Mission to hide from and take only evasive actions against other submarines, listening devices, and torpedoes that may be tracking you in the Alpha Cordillera area. Take all defensive actions necessary, but no offensive actions during mission. Ship's log to be electronically recorded at all times. Mission to conclude by signal of submarine broaching surface, or after fourteen days, at fourteen hundred (14:00) on April 17.
> Commander of Naval Operations:
> *James T. Watkins*
> Admiral James Watkins

With a puzzled look on his face, Maple handed the sheet back to Smith, who turned over the single page, searching for more. But the other side was blank. The captain held the paper up to the light, and immediately recognized the imprinted Navy watermark, the final confirmation that what he had read was indeed from the Commander of Naval Operations. Orders don't come from much higher than that.

Smith replied to the questioning eyes of his second officer by simply shrugging. "We've got a job to do, but damned if I can guess what it is."

"Now I know what a sitting duck feels like, captain," Maple said as he looked hard at his superior.

"Or a rabbit outside his hole," the captain replied as he folded the paper, tucked it in his shirt pocket, and headed to the Officer's Mess. "Call the others. Five minutes."

Did the captain know these were the orders when they set sail? Was he really as much in the dark as he seemed? Thought Lieutenant Maple.

To Captain Smith's junior officers, five minutes meant four-and-a-half, and all had shown up immediately when they heard Maple's call on the intercom. As the last of the seven men entered the room, Captain Smith was just pulling seven sheets from the portable copier, the one designed by the ship's builder to do two things: electronically copy, then forget. Its heat-transmitting carbon spools were volatile and left no imprint from previous runs. A submarine is a controlled environment, but word gets around. And sometimes a captain didn't want word to get around. At least not before he was ready.

Maple closed the door. Some of the officers had already finished reading the orders, and raised their questioning faces just as the lieutenant had done five minutes earlier in the captain's quarters.

"Amazing lack of detail, wouldn't you say gentlemen?" Smith asked, rhetorically, pouring himself a cup of coffee from the bar at the back of the officers' mess. His staff officers knew better than to answer. It wasn't really a question. "Have a seat."

It was a short meeting. The captain explained that the sub would proceed with strict silent running rules. The officers were to return to their battle stations and brief their immediate crews. All loose items were to be stowed or secured. If the captain saw one loose pen, or untied shoe, or a coffee mug too close to the edge of a table there'd be hell to pay. "Most cruise orders I get are at least three pages long. This was just one. So we'll have to make up the other two. In the meantime, no noise and no questions. Your guess is as good as mine, and right now I'm not even going to try to guess. Best thing we can do is what they told us: Run silent. And hide."

The Arctic under-ice formations mimic the mountainous ocean floor of the Alpha Cordillera region of the North Pole. Large, irregular shaped stalactite ice-forms point down from the surface toward rippled mounds below. What little light there is is absorbed in long, undulating shadows that dissolve into the fathoms of ocean deep below. An eerie sight for most. Submarines don't have windows because of the tremendous pressures on the hull. And it's a good thing they don't. Seeing those haunting shadows would only further stress the crew.

Captain Smith looked down peering over the ocean charts laid out on the light table in the center of the bridge. The charts showed the curled lines of currents, thermo clines, and the last-known positions of ice formations. But ice formations change, and the sonar operators had been given strict orders for constant vigilance to the sonar signature of the terrain. They were the eyes, and more importantly, the ears of the ship. Theirs was the job of keeping the ship clear of the jagged ice. Too close to one of those mammoth icicles and the submarine gets a gash that cripples it. Just close enough is where the captain wanted them to be.

Problem is a submarine captain doesn't always know from which direction the threat is coming. The wall of ice a ship might use to hide behind could turn out to highlight its position to an oncoming threat from the opposite direction. One never knows until the last minute. And then it's too late.

*   *   *

Two days later, the dim green lights of the Hawkbill's bridge illuminated the crew staring at gauges and adjusting control levers to keep the ship quiet-running between alternating depths—from just under the ice ceiling to a maximum of three-hundred feet below. The submarine was at three-hundred feet, conditions that relieved the sonar man from his intense focus of looking out for unexpected stalactites at the ceiling. But no matter what depth, forty-eight hours is a long time to run silent, and the fatigue and stress showed on the faces of the crew. Junior officers were more frequently chewing out their crewmen for small mistakes, and the captain was starting to notice.

Capt. Smith stood over the helmsman, pleased that they'd hit a smooth gap in ice formations. Smooth meant the crew could ease up, maybe sit back in their seats and stretch muscles sore from the tension. One could get use to this, the captain thought, maybe a couple more days and—

"Torpedo pings, Captain—approximately four thousand yards and closing from aft-starboard quadrant!" It was Grahams, the primary sonar operator. He was only 28, but the captain had learned to rely on his judgment, and his reflexes. He was young and very smart. And he never raised his voice unless there was reason.

This was a reason.

"Port heading forty-five degrees!" the captain shouted to the helmsman. "ALL AHEAD FULL!" Captain Smith quietly cursed himself for his complacent reverie a half-second before. "Let's get back to that ice cave and lose those pings."

The ship trembled in reaction to turned control levers, its single screw accelerating to the maximum. A sub always responded slower than the adrenaline that fueled the crew, a maddening difference that they never got used to.

"If we can lose that torpedo before it switches to attack speed, we may have a chance." The captain wanted to believe what he had just said.

Capt. Smith turned back to the sonar man, "Grahams, any idea who launched that torpedo? You haven't sighted any subs in that location, have you?"

"No, Sir!" Grahams snapped back. "No subs in that area and definitely no surface ships. The ice cap is much too thick up there. That torpedo just appeared. Like out of nowhere!"

The Hawkbill was turning hard to the port heading and the crew on the bridge now leaned in to the new pitch as the floor shifted beneath their feet. They had been through this maneuver many times before, but never with a torpedo attack from out of nowhere. Adrenaline infused their blood and their senses heightened.

"Damn!" Capt. Smith shouted, beads of sweat forming across his forehead. "Give me more speed, helmsman! Those ice forms were plenty big enough to hide in. They can't be that far back!"

Training and experience told the captain that torpedo sonar pings bounce differently off of ice than his boat. He knew if he could get his submarine behind the ice forms before the torpedo locked on he might be able to break trail.

The submarine continued its turn toward the submerged ice cave in the distance, increasing speed while still jerking in erratic angles to the torpedo track. But the torpedo was too close to be evaded. It maneuvered with the sub, correcting course to its ping returns. The mouse was chasing the cat, and the cat was losing ground. Both disappeared into the ocean's darkness.

CHAPTER 3
Putting the Team Together

Nine months earlier, at 10:30 am on the Monday after his meeting with Secretary Lehman, Alex Trinola was late for work. He was speeding in and out of traffic in his decked out Porsche. Alex had paid extra for turbo-charging and he was using it now. He hit the brakes as he bumped over the entrance ramp to the parking lot of the Naval Ocean Systems Center, coasted up to the gate, and in one coordinated motion he eased the car to a stop as his hand held his pass out the driver's side window. Three minutes later he was walking double time past the secretary next to his office of Torpedo Design and Engineering. "Morning. They're all in there?"

Trinola's secretary looked up, mildly annoyed at her boss's tardiness. "Yes, except for Jack and Len who are just finishing up a high pressure run in the test pits. I sent Rob over to get them."

So I'm not the only one late, Trinola thought to himself as he hurried past his secretary's desk. "Ok, send them in as soon as they get here. I'll be in the conference room."

At the test pits, engineers Jack Boncare and Len Morini couldn't care less that they were late for a meeting. They peered through thick plexiglass windows at a torpedo engine running on a test stand. Its high frequency noise was loud, very loud, even outside the enclosure. Jack rotated the throttle control and watched the RPM needle creep toward red line.

"It meets the design goal, Jack, why push it any further?" asked Len, not once looking up from the gauge.

Jack rotated the throttle a bit more, moving the needle beyond the red line. "Judas Priest, Jack, what are you—" A loud explosion filled the ears of the engineers, with an almost concussive effect. Len and Jack reflexively held their arms over their faces and ducked as the high-pressure pump exploded, sending metal bouncing off the four-inch plexiglass partition, and popping the pressure relief fittings in the ceiling. Outside, the immediate sky filled with gray cylinders of exhaust. Inside, crimson flashes of ignited fuel and billowing smoke filled the chamber, obscuring the view of what was left of the device.

"Damn!" Len shouted, as vent fans automatically cleared the chamber, revealing hundreds of pieces of his mechanical masterpiece scattered across the room. A single bar of metal rested on what was left of the engine bulkhead, a vague suggestion of the fuel pump that had been there.

"Jack, why'd you have to push it so far?! You never know when to stop!" Len shouted, just as Rob O'Nerhy entered the control room and interjected, unhelpfully, "Hey, my banjo strings do the same thing when I tighten 'em too much. 'Course, they only cost a couple bucks apiece. I figure what you two just blew up cost Uncle Sam a little more."

Ignoring O'Nerhy, Jack turned to his colleague, "Sorry, Len, but now we know its limits."

"Was that another one of those 'unknown significant tests'?" O'Nerhly asked, the mocking tone clear in his voice. "Don't answer that. Hey, Trinola wants to see us guys in his conference room right now. Something big, I'm thinkin."

As Rob and Jack both looked back at the charred remains on the test bench, Jack remarked, with a sigh, "Well, I guess we've done enough damage for one morning." They turned back in unison and preceded Len out the door. Five minutes later they were in the conference room, although one person shy.

"Where's Len?" Trinola asked, looking up from his folder and not succeeding in hiding his impatience.

"He was just here with us," Rob said, turning around and walking back out the door.

"He's probably crying in his office," Jack offered, taking a seat. "I just blew up his fuel pump."

Back in his office, Len sat at his desk, completely forgetting the meeting he was supposed to attend. Navy design documents he had personally authored were scattered in front of him, along with the design textbook he had just completed. Rolled up drawings seemed to reach for him from every crevice in the room, protruding like un-pruned tree limbs that filled the spaces between the framed degrees from California universities, gold-leaf design awards from the Navy, and several prestigious patent awards. Len's achievement plaques would be impressive to any first-time visitor to his office, except for the complete and utter mess that surrounded them.

A slender man, weighing only about 130 pounds, Len appeared frail. What Len lacked in physical strength was more than compensated by his mental abilities, as his office accolades declared. But at this moment he was frustrated as he stooped over his drafting table gazing at the drawings of the fuel pump that just blew up. He corrected himself, 'that Jack just blew up.'

Rob quietly entered Len's office and stared at him for a moment, contemplating the words he should say to bring Len back to the present. After a moment, he barked "Ha! Another revolting development, but nothing compared to the next project Trinola has for us, I bet! We better go and find what it's all about."

Len sighed, remembering his duty, and stepped from behind his drafting table. He followed his colleague down the hall.

Back in the conference room, Alex Trinola had already started his briefing. The tone of his voice lent a sense of intensity to the room. "While we're waiting for Len and Rob, let me introduce Mr. Ross Spiry. He is an analyst from Washington, D.C. I met him in John Lehman's office last week, when the Secretary gave us the go-ahead for the program. Ross is going with us to keep Lehman informed and help you, Kent, with recording the data."

Spiry nodded his head to those in attendance, all of whom noted his impeccable dress. A fortyish man with a slim build, Spiry looked out of place in a building filled with uniformed military and civilian engineers, most of whom wore their own type of uniform: rumpled pants, scuffed shoes, and short-sleeved shirts with bulging pockets. Spiry looked out of his element. And he smelled of political influence and power.

Trinola proceeded to introduce his colleges to Spiry.

"This is Kent Richerson, our electronics engineer and his counterpart, Greg Bounds. Greg is an expert in torpedo strategic patterns and programs."

"This is Jack Boncare. Some call him 'Mr. Power Punch.' One of our more aggressive torpedo test engineers at the center."

"And this is Gary Tercar, our civilian contractor who will manufacture the launcher Len will be designing. He'll be going to the Arctic with us, too."

There was a short interruption as the door opened. Trinola scowled as Len and Rob walked into the conference room, Len holding a steaming cup of coffee which he apparently felt he needed enough to stop and get on the way. Len sat down. He took a quick glance around the conference table, noting the four other engineers he knew, and a fifth man. Len had never seen him before.

Alex continued.

"Good. Close the door Rob and take a seat. Mr. Ross Spiry, this is Rob O'Nerhy, technician and logistics expert; and this is Len Morini, the engineer who will be designing our mobile torpedo launcher."

"Len's probably a little frustrated right now because Jack just pushed the design limit on his fuel pump. But he'll get over it with this next project."

Trinola continued the briefing, including how he had met with the Secretary the previous week, where he first heard about the project, the project so important as to change the course of the Cold War. "Our project involves secret operations and an extraordinary design and logistic challenge. We are to launch our torpedoes from atop the Arctic ice pack." The engineers looked around the room at one another, except for Len, who took out a pad of paper and jotted down a quick note.

"Our team of engineers will not only have to create new launch and test equipment, they will actually be involved in every aspect of development, deployment, and program operations at the North Pole. And above all, they'll have to do it under stringent security.

"Our team members have to be ready for deployment in less than nine months, and be shipped out with all the hardware. We'll be gone from our families for at least a month."

Trinola added, "On the flight back from the Pentagon, Admiral Gooluc asked me if I thought my people could get it all together and do the job. He gave me four days to give him an answer, but I told the

Admiral I'd get back to him in three." Trinola, always pushing the envelope, looked around the room for affirmation. But only neutral faces gazed back at him. Engineers are not fast decision-makers. It's not in their genetic code.

*   *   *

Personality Players

Alex Trinola was always confident, from his earliest days as a torpedo technician at the Pasadena Naval laboratory in 1968. He quickly transitioned to a test program operator, moved into coordinator and then manager at the Naval Center, San Diego. In every position he earned the rewards of exemplary hard work and self-sacrificial loyalty. His years of experience as a top-notch torpedo technician and gifted manager had earned him the respect of his department, and certainly every engineer in the room. But at that moment, they needed more information.

He stretched out his bulging forearms over the table, and clapped his thick hands together, punctuating the moment, preparing to speak. He knew this assignment to the North Pole would either bring him greater success, or break him. He shook off his personal thoughts and looked back at his engineers.

"I have chosen each of you in this room because I know you have the special abilities to accomplish this task. Even though we only have a few months to do it, I know we can."

"We live in precarious times, gentlemen, especially with the recent submarine buildup of the Soviets to the north. All of you are cleared for top secret programs and what I am about to describe is exactly that. You are not to discuss any of this beyond this room. And pretty soon, we'll be about as far away from this room as is possible. We're going to the top of the world."

Trinola continued describing the details of the program the Admiral had given him, together with the scribblings he came up with during the sleepless night before. The test program would involve launching torpedoes through the Arctic ice cap against America's own submarines to finally determine just how capable and accurate they were. The team would either silence the bragging submarine skippers who claimed they could hide and/or evade torpedoes behind ice formations, or once and for all prove the torpedoes' capabilities to be true. The torps would either find the subs, or be blinded and confused by the submarines' evasive tactics or by the naturally hostile and uncooperative ice formations.

Pleased that most of the men in the room had been scribbling steadily, Trinola concluded his comments with a specific directive to one man. "Len, I want you to design a mobile launcher that can fire-up and send our torpedoes through a hole in the ice toward our submarines."

Len stopped scribbling and looked up. A slow smile creased his face as he considered the challenge, only to darken as he remembered the explosion that just occurred. "It sounds possible, but the schedule is pretty tight," he offered. "I'll need priority supply lines and expedited requisitions. I'll need most of the test boosters in our inventory, and probably—

Trinola held up his hand. "Whatever you need Len. It's yours."

"But will the sub captains be in on the drill?"

Trinola smiled, and nodded his head. "You bet, they'll know—especially when they hear those torpedoes coming after them! But if we are successful; if your launcher is successful, they'll never know from where."

As Len Morini considered this last statement, Trinola quietly reviewed the reasons he was giving Len this once-in-a-career challenge. Len was a master design engineer, a civil servant hired at the Pasadena Lab, just a few days before Trinola. He was one of the Center's most creative design engineers, which is why Trinola chose him. Len thought outside the box, beyond the slide rule. But that could also be a major character flaw, and Trinola had thought long about whether this independent thinker—who had never appreciated military command structure—would really be the right fit. Trinola remembered one division head who had called Len a "prima donna," charged words in a military environment. Trinola's team needed to work together to succeed, and he had worried about Len. In the end, though, Len's skills and experience outweighed the personality concerns. Keeping the team working well together was not Len's job, after all. It was Trinola's.

Trinola snapped back to the business at hand. "Len, that launcher has to be not only mobile, but as quiet as possible. That's a technical challenge, but not an overwhelming one. We're not reinventing the wheel here, but adapting a lot of work that you all have already done in other projects. But there IS something that we have to especially consider, and it may even be more important than the engineering expertise we all bring. And it's this: Everyone on this team has to work together, from design concepts to tests and logistics. No one can be a prima donna here," Trinola winced at his own mental slip, shook his head, and continued, "if ANY of you have problems, ANY problems, you come see me about it. It's my job to keep us together, on time, on target, and civil with one another."

Len nodded in recognition, hoping nobody else remembered that he, in particular, had a history of being the nonconformist. The other men at the table appeared in agreement with Trinola's words. They knew he was talking mainly about Len, most likely the weakest link in any team effort, but also the guy who could "think" his way out of any technical problem that might arise.

Changing the focus, Trinola said, "Jack, tests and logistics are a big part of this program, and you and Rob will have to make sure everything that is ordered, packaged and shipped will be on time. In fact, there is very little room for mistakes. So, I want you two guys to come up with the best checklists you have ever devised."

Jack Boncare, the youngest engineer on the team, nodded in agreement. A dedicated weight lifter, Jack was a physically aggressive and disciplined guy. He got things done. He was experienced in all aspects of test engineering, from designing hardware to conducting actual test programs. Even if it meant causing the occasional explosion, Jack was a whiz at testing. Jack was a team player, too, enthusiastic about meeting expectations, pushing himself and his colleagues. A bit gruff and arrogant at times, this big-chested Italian was also fun to be around, verbal about his observations, and occasionally sarcastic. His natural can-do temperament encouraged everyone, from the kids he coached on Little League to his colleagues at work.

Trinola glanced at Rob O'Nerhy, to his left, who had been sitting silently, making few notes, and generally observing the proceedings. O'Nerhy was one of the most compliant members of the team, an asset to such an undertaking. But his compliance was less important than his other qualities. Rob was not only skilled in logistics, but had the uncanny ability to find and purchase practically anything overnight. Trained as a draftsman and technician in the Navy, he had years of experience in assembling torpedoes. But one of his assets to *this* team was assembling all the tools and accessories needed for the program. Trinola was confident that O'Nerhy's detail-oriented nature would be perfect for anticipating the many things needed on the Arctic ice: Kevlar vests, specifically-sized pairs of gloves, face-shields, wool beanies, shaded ski glasses for those extra bright days on the ice, ski mobiles operable to 40 degrees below zero, and even plastic-housed wristwatches so "we won't have metal freezing against our skin." And extra sets of everything.

"Hey Alex, you can put me in charge of entertainment, too. I think I'll requisition some VHS and video equipment so we won't get bored during those long Arctic nights. Sound of Music okay with everybody?"

Chuckles bubbled from most of the men in the room. Spiry was the lone exception, who for the entire meeting had sat neutrally with his hands clasped together on the table in front of him. Then Kent Richerson, the head electronics engineer on the project, asked a serious question. "Alex, sounds like we need to modify the computer program for the torpedoes, right? One that will not only prevent target collisions, but one that can adjust the ping frequencies for ice-density bounce—just in case. After all, we don't want our torpedoes hitting our subs!"

Trinola nodded. "We will also have to work out the minimum turn-away distance; maybe something like 200 yards or so. I know that's 100 yards less than the usual distance for turn-away, but Lehman is asking for the minimum our torps can tolerate and still avoid hitting subs. Lehman doesn't want the sub skippers becoming complacent."

"Jesus! I guess he wants quick adrenaline reactions from those skippers," Richerson exclaimed. "200 yards seems a tight avoidance turn for our torpedoes when they are at attack speed, especially considering today's subs are almost a football field long."

"Do we have time to do some torpedo tests at maximum turn rate at maximum speed?" Richerson asked quickly.

The "we" he was referring to was Greg Bounds, the other 'electronics type' on the team and a crack torpedo strategist from Seattle. He smiled at the acknowledgement, but didn't take his eyes off his notepad, on which was written the number 200. Two hundred yards was well within a torpedo's lock-on and maximum attack-speed setting, and at that distance most sub commanders would already be making the sign of the cross over their chests as they braced for impact—just a few seconds away from Amen. He wondered if they might back that off a bit, to minimize the number of unnecessary heart attacks, or at least cause fewer crew members to wet their pants. More questions later, he told himself.

Trinola replied, "Lehman's office is asking for our recommendations right now. No time for actual tests, so you'll have to rely on some pretty heavy calculations. Of course the sub skippers will undoubtedly want large turn-away distances. Even though they probably think our torpedoes will never find them. They will want the greatest escape-distance they can get. But you guys figure out what we can get away with. Try to get 200 yards for Lehman, even if that means backing down slightly on the maximum attack speed. Hearing one of our torps still closing at 200 yards will cause those skippers to cry 'OH MOMMA'—whatever the attack speed!"

Bounds smiled. His earlier concern for the sub captains' emotional states was replaced by the challenge implicit in the skippers' confidence at avoiding detection. He saw that as a challenge, and he never backed down from a challenge. Don't get TOO confident, my captains, he said to himself. We shall see. Then he added, aloud, "But no matter what the turn-away distance, I'm sure our torpedoes will find them, since we are going to program our babies for both snake and circular search patterns to be most efficient."

Trinola continued, "I am sure some at the Pentagon will be hesitant to fire torpedoes against our own subs, just like Admiral Rickover always was. But, since we'll be telling them everything up-front—a benefit for us, just in case anything goes wrong—we won't get blamed for holding out information. Plus, we'll get bragging rites at the pub after this is all over. Sub captains will be buying, of course."

Kent chimed in, "I think you're right about one thing: It's a good thing Rickover is not still around. He would never allow such torpedo tests against 'his' nuclear subs! Especially at reduced turn-away distances!"

"Yeah," Trinola added, "Rickover always wanted every detail shared with his submariners. Frankly, I wouldn't be surprised if Lehman helped instigate Rickover's retirement to minimize the flack for these tests against our own subs. I heard Lehman is a pretty strong-willed character. He sure seemed that way when I met him last week—always in charge, doing most of the talking."

A disturbed look came over Trinola's face. "Come to think of it, Lehman didn't really share too much detail about what the skippers would be told. I wonder—"

"We'll leave the politics to you, sir," Kent said, "But as far as our new technology goes, it probably won't make any difference when they see what our torpedoes can do. Our agile lightweight Mark 46 torpedoes have on-board computers programmed with the latest logistics that can decipher and search out even the most elusive subs. And, our torps can do all that in nanoseconds."

Looking up from his note pad, where he had jotted down a quick calculation, Len joined in, "The other thing is they won't know where the torpedoes are coming from. They'll just seem to appear out of nowhere!"

"That's right. That's the big variable," added Jack. "Are we going to be launching torpedoes from different locations at the same time?"

"From different locations," replied Trinola, "but not simultaneously. That would make tracking very difficult, not to mention the chance of torpedoes targeting each other. We'll have to play a little with timing consecutive launches."

The minds of the engineers in the room raced ahead—multiple shots, different locations, surface launches. None of this had ever been done before. This will be interesting, maybe historic, they thought together. Engineers didn't care about history, only the next insurmountable problem to solve or the next technical challenge to meet. History is written by others, by people who look back. The people in this room knew they were a whole different group altogether. They looked ahead.

"Come to think of it, what's going to do the tracking?" Asked Kent. "I guess we want something faster than the onboard torpedo recorders. If we rely on them, we won't know what they've done until the torpedoes are recovered."

Trinola spoke quickly, already anticipating that question: "Command has arranged Navy Seals to lay down an array of hydrophones even before the Arctic ice camp is settled in and the submarines arrive on-site. These listening devices will be hanging from holes in the ice sheet at around the ninety-foot depth. At least that's what they're shooting for. The hydrophone array will give you the tracking you'll need, in real time. You'll have Mr. Spiry here to help with all the recording equipment."

The engineers around the table looked over at Spiry, realizing that he had been in the room the whole time. He had not spoken, not really moved, as they thought about it. The briefing and their furious scribbles had occupied their attention. They now gazed at Spiry, expecting a reply to Trinola's statement. None was given.

Trinola continued, "Kent, you, Greg, and Spiry will be in the communications hut during tests, seeing firsthand what's happening. You'll also be talking to us out at our launching locations, keeping us informed."

"Sounds good," said Kent, still expecting a response from Spiry, who instead gazed steadily at Trinola, his hands resting on the table. Who *was* this guy, thought the engineers.

CHAPTER 4

The Ultimate Game of Warfare

Six months later, April 12, 1986, forty mile-an-hour gusts of wind were pelting the torpedo launch team. Alex Trinola, Jack Boncare, Rob O'Nerhy, Gary Tercar and two navy divers were one mile due west of the Arctic ice camp. Bracing against the elements, they struggled to coordinate their movements to lower a 500-pound torpedo through a large hole in the surface of the ice. This particular type of Mk 46 torpedo—classed as a "light weight" anti-sub torpedo—had been launched successfully from various aircraft and ship platforms for many years. But this Mk 46 was different. For the first time in torpedo engineering history, a torpedo had been programmed to launch from the surface of the Arctic ice pack, to seek out and attack hidden subs before it returned to its launch depth for recovery. The warhead section did not contain explosives. The torpedo had been programmed to end its close rate at precisely 200 yards from impact and then turn away. At least, that was the hope.

Trinola and his men were dressed in dark blue, cold-weather Kevlar suits. This gear was perfect for mountain climbing and exploring, but less useful when holding a release cable with one hand while signaling with the other. Jack and Rob steadied the dual-claw launcher hanging from the large quadrupod that Gary steadied over a rectangular hole cut into the ice. Two divers in black, heavy-weight wet suits were in the hole. They helped each other remove the last large ice block before getting out of the water that already began to refreeze.

Gusts of wind howled around them. They struggled to lower the launcher with its blunt-nosed torpedo into the ragged-edged hole and dark blue water waiting below. Finally, they managed to lower it through the hole, steadying the bulky device into position. A signal from Jack indicated the launcher was fully submerged and ready. Trinola pulled the release cable and to his relief the torpedo screw turned and the launcher vibrated as the prop spun up. One second later the torpedo moved free of its bracing and disappeared into the black water.

"Torpedo number 14 away!" Trinola yelled into his WT-headset, "Mark confirmation, Kent! Do you read?"

Kent's metallic voice burst from the walkie-talkie, cutting through the wind. "Yes, Kent here—confirmation." Looking down at his monitor in the communication tent a few miles away, Kent could see the blip indicator moving. "Mark now, 11:16 and tracking torpedo 14!"

The sound of an approaching snowmobile caused Trinola and his men to turn. Len slid the two-track vehicle to a stop and jumped off quickly. "Sorry I am late," Len cried out, shouting through the storm that, despite the noise, could not muffle the apologetic tone in his voice. His goggles didn't obscure the sheepish look on his face as he yelled, "I thought you wouldn't start without me. It's my launcher, after all!"

"Yeah, well I know you don't have a valid excuse," Trinola angrily replied, moving away from the hole as his colleagues pulled the launcher from the water. He wasn't in any mood to listen to the reason for Len's tardiness. "It's just lucky nothing went wrong with your launcher!

"This can't happen again, Len," Trinola shouted through the howling wind. "We are a team up here, and every team member must be involved. The whole program may rely on any one of us. Got that?"

Trinola moved his walkie-talkie to his lips, not waiting for Len's reply, which was lost in the Arctic wind anyway. Len's excuse of Bible study and prayer for the success of the team would not have satisfied even the Catholic in his boss. Trinola could only think of the immediate task.

"Kent, any update on torps 13 and 14?" Trinola shouted into the mouthpiece.

"Kent here. Number 13 just switched to secondary ping rate against the Hawkbill. It's closing in at thirty-two degrees. And number 14 is in a circular search just below where you launched it."

*   *   *

Onboard the USS Hawkbill, sonar man Grahams called out, "Torpedo ping rate just switched. Four thousand yards and closing Captain!"

"Where's that ice cave we passed awhile ago?!" Capt. Smith shouted back, his voice rising in alarm.

"About three hundred yards…southwest fifty-three degrees at twenty-foot ceiling, Captain."

Capt. Smith turned to the helmsman and called out, "Forty degrees port and up to ninety feet…fifteen incline, Clancy."

"Forty degrees port to bearing southwest fifty-three, fifteen degrees incline, Captain!" Clancy replied, struggling to do his duty and remain calm.

Captain Smith leaned onto the back of his sonar man's chair, watching the screen, and breathing hard. "This is going to be real close, Grahams, so tune your sonar to fine setting. We don't want to plow into anything."

"Doing it right now, Captain," replied Grahams, anticipating the order. What else could we do anyway, he thought to himself, but then shook off the sarcasm. Sarcasm is a luxury for those not being pursued by explosive devices 200 feet below Arctic ice.

*   *   *

Torpedo pings were bouncing rapidly off the sub's hull now, an audible sound the crew transferred directly to their guts. They listened in fear as the pings continued, getting louder by the second. With the captain and sonar man focused on the growing blip on the screen the helmsman guided the Hawkbill toward the open entrance of a cave formed by clustered ice formations, like an inverted canyon. The pings quickened as the torpedo closed.

Scraping against long, thin stalactite formations, the Hawkbill shook as ice broke off and floated to the ice-sheet ceiling above. The crew braced themselves as momentary jerks impeded the subs forward motion and larger chunks of ice were ripped away from their ceiling foundations. The noise of crunching ice spiked into louder, resonating frequencies of the fast approaching torpedo.

Grahams cringed as he turned down his earphones, but just as quickly turned them back up again. He couldn't afford to miss the frequency change when the sub's pings outlined the entrance to the ice cave. Grahams still did not know where the chasing torpedo was. He kept switching from the close to far settings of the sonar system, trying to triangulate its location.

Luckily, and as yet unknown to the captain or crew, the Hawkbill was beating the odds. While the torpedo closed in on its target, the sub was maneuvering and had aligned itself into a perfect track toward the vestibule of the ice-cave. If it could reach the cave in time, it would be shielded from the oncoming torpedo.

*   *   *

Grahams adjusted his sonar screen to pick up more detail and called out, "Ice cave thirty yards, Captain, up fifteen feet. Looks good—open-bottom cave. Entrance real good. Easy access."

Capt. Smith turned to the helmsman again, "Easy, up three degrees, Clancy. Get us up and in there NOW. Steady as she goes."

"Steady as she goes, sir."

"Starboard, five degrees!" Grahams yelled out.

Capt. Smith repeated the order to Clancy while the submarine brushed against more ice at the entrance of the cave. The needles of Clancy's gauges vibrated in erratic response and Smith and his men grabbed any surface they could reach to steady their positions. Glancing at their captain for reassurance, the crew saw reflected in his face their own fear: maybe seeking shelter in this ice cave is more dangerous than facing that torpedo. After all, this was just an exercise, wasn't it? What else COULD it be?

The sub trembled as it struck another ice wall, but this time the ice didn't give way. It was a solid wall. The sub careened starboard, sending the crew in the bow to the floor, and others headlong into bulkheads, gauges, valves, and other equipment. Arms and faces came up bloodied as the men returned to their seats and stations. A frightened yeoman recited a prayer as he grabbed at his chair and crawled back up to his console.

The helmsman struggled with the wheel as he corrected the

Hawkbill's momentum to starboard as it entered the ice cave. Grahams yelled, "Torpedo closing at nine hundred yards, Captain... eight hundred yards... seven hundred yards!"

The frequency of the torpedo pings increased as the unseen weapon closed. Men braced themselves again, their minds reeling with the thought of what it would feel like to die in a submarine. Stone-faced instructors had taught them early on that a breach in the hull of a submerged submarine produced such a fast and massive pressure change, its crush would be instantaneous, and therefore painless. Doomed submariners didn't drown, the students had been surprised to learn. They are crushed to death by the pressure of millions of tons of ocean water suddenly breaching the vessel.

"Attack frequency switch, Captain!" Grahams was almost standing now, his body subconsciously trying to distance itself from the growing orbs on the screen. "Six hundred yards...five hundred yards...four hundred yards!"

The torpedo was at full attack speed following the electronic return signature of the submarine. Then the returns were interrupted. The Hawkbill eased to a stop inside the ice cave as the pings on the cabin speaker diminished. Then they stopped. No one spoke, until Grahams whispered, "I...I think we've broken trail, captain."

At 300 yards from the Hawkbill the torpedo received its last return ping. The Hawkbill had indeed broken trail. At this distance a standard test torp would have turned away and shut down, but the ICE-X torpedo decelerated. Its computer switched to the slower search ping rate. Following its protocol the torp proceeded to snake to the right and left, its receivers "listening" for a moving target again. As it scanned the entrance of the ice cave, it got two return pings from the tail of the submarine, still shifting within the ice cave. The torpedo turned and locked onto its target, switching to attack ping rate again. It sped toward the entrance of the cave.

"Ohmygod, Captain! It found us!" Grahams cried out, as new pings became audible. "I don't believe it! It's less than 250 yards away. A test torpedo would've turned away by now!"

With shock on their faces, the crew braced themselves for the inevitable. The fear was palpable as adrenaline provoked stomach acid and dilated pupils. To a man, they waited for death. Then silence— dead silence.

"I don't believe it, Sir. It looks like it broke trail again." Grahams slumped in his chair, bewildered, relieved, emotionally spent. Still diligent, he continued to adjust the volume of the sonar speakers. He expected the pings to return again, as if some sadistic machine was toying with them before tearing the ship in half and sending them all into the frozen deep.

*   *   *

Speeding toward the Hawkbill, the torpedo turned at the entrance of the cave, its last sonar return confirmed it had reached the 200 yard separation limit. As programmed, it made a 90-degree turn while shutting down and heading back toward the surface.

Inside the communications hut, Kent, Greg, and Ross Spiry had been listening to the underwater drama, deciphering the pings, monitoring the distance returns, and imagining the crews' reaction. The whole time, their tape machines recorded every ping.

Kent pressed the send button on his radio, "Trinola, sounds like number 13 just got two acquires before tripping its two-hundred-yard turn away. That's our fourth success against the Hawkbill—five against the USS Ray, and four against the USS Archerfish."

"One-hundred percent, so far!" Kent exclaimed, barely containing his excitement, and his pride. "We're thirteen for thirteen!"

"Good news," Trinola acknowledged. He was still outside, still in the cold, and trying hard to share the feeling of success as he brushed off the ice crystals accumulated on his walkie-talkie. "Kind of ironic that the 'Devil Boat 666' couldn't beat the spell of lucky number 13 torpedo. I can see the headlines now! So what's happening with number 14?"

"It got one spurious acquisition," Kent's voice replied through the walkie-talkie speaker, "But now looks like it's in circular search mode and...ah, checking again."

Kent dialed up the volume of the tracking receiver. "From where it is right now, number 14 should be picking up the Archerfish any moment."

*   *   *

The USS Archerfish was cruising at two hundred fifty feet, comfortably below any known stalactite formations. Many of its sailors

32

sat at a mess table in the dim red lighting, clutching coffee cups with USS Archerfish logos. The crew was discussing the situation with Lieutenant Commander Reigle, when someone asked, "So how many other subs are involved in these tests?"

Lieut. Commander Reigle, looked up from his coffee cup, where he had been watching the ripples on the surface caused by the sub's engine vibrations, "Seems like there are two others. We got a positive profile on the USS Ray and one on the USS Hawkbill before it seemed to disappear."

"What do you mean?"

"Well, Ears said he heard some torpedo pings just before losing Hawkbill's profile behind an ice formation," explained Reigle. Standing up to stretch his tired body, he added, "So I don't know whether Hawkbill's hiding ploy worked, or the torpedo got within its turn-away distance as it is programmed to do. These are just games, you know."

Another crew member at the table said, "Well, that was my guess, Commander—just games—but then Ears told someone that torpedo got much closer to the Hawkbill than the usual turn-away distance. He's never seen a test torpedo get that close. We all get nervous when we hear those damn pings on our hull. What Ears said has started us thinking, maybe these torps aren't dummies after all."

Reigle looked up from his coffee cup, knowing he'd need to employ his leadership skills and reassure an unexpectedly edgy crewman. "Look, they're just tests, that's all. And if not, well, you still shouldn't worry. Our Captain has been pretty successful in using ice forms to evade those torpedoes, even before their abort distance."

"Do you or the Captain know what that turn-away distance is?" another crew member asked, his voice echoing his fellow crew member's anxiety.

"Well no, they didn't tell us that. I just assume we're doing better than those damn torpedoes can do. We have evaded four torps without any problem so far. They can't see us behind the ice walls. So let's stay with our experience instead of rumor, for God's sakes!"

Confident he had put his crew's questions—and nerves—to rest, the young Lieutenant Commander permitted himself an inner smile. He swigged the last of his coffee and walked over to the dish trays before heading to the bridge.

Reigle was 36 years old and had been second in command of

the Archerfish for the past six years. Raised in Connecticut, close to where the Archerfish was built, Reigle carried "a sense of destiny," that connected with being on "his boat" for the honor and security of his nation. He tried to instill that sense of honor in the crew, and that in turn earned him their respect. The crew also knew he had been on the Archerfish longer than most of them, and for that matter, longer than the Captain.

The Archerfish was the same 600 class submarine as the Hawkbill and Ray. Thirty-two feet wide and ninety-seven yards long, this latest class—Sturgeon-class—of subs carried Harpoon missiles, Tomahawk cruise missiles, and torpedoes. It was the largest class attack sub of the U.S. fleet. The Ray was the oldest, built in 1967. The Hawkbill was christened in February 1971 (keeping its 666 number after much controversy). The Archerfish was christened later that same year in December. Each had been retrofitted with improved sonar equipment for Arctic voyages. That retrofit, along with their experienced crews, gave them an advantage over other submarines when it came to evading torpedoes, especially under the ice at the top of the world. At least that was the claim.

Captain Koresh had skippered the Archerfish for four years, three of which had involved exercises at the North Pole. He had evaded subs and their test torpedoes before. But in Arctic waters evasion becomes more complex with the addition of ice floes, polynyas—open areas of water surrounded by sea ice—larger temperature gradients, and huge ice formations that affect water currents under the ice pack. However, Captain Koresh's five-nine stature, large compared to most submariners, and his similarly commanding presence on the bridge, always presented the level of confidence his crew needed to establish the Archerfish's notable success.

*   *   *

Just as Lieut. Commander Reigle boarded the bridge, the Archerfish's sonar man, called out. "Capt. Koresh, I am hearing some intermittent pings in the distance, about... Wait. Could be bearing one-thirty-five."

A slight pinging was heard coming through a sonar speaker as Ears adjusted the volume.

"How far away?" his captain asked, moving toward Ears' station.

"Hard to say Captain... maybe three thousand yards?"

The captain turned back to his helmsman, and quickly spoke. "All stop, silent glide, ten degrees up. Let's melt into that ice ceiling."

The Archerfish glided toward the surface, its ballast tanks slowly bleeding out water to lighten the load. The sub leveled off just beneath the ceiling and in between several jagged ice formations. Slowing to a crawl, it came to rest, its bulk floating like a silent shadow against the surrounding stalactites of ice.

In a whisper, the captain commanded: "All running systems down. Now!"

As the steady hums of the various instruments on the bridge ebbed to silence, the only sounds were the torpedo pings from Ears' speakers. Staring at each other in the glow of the red light, the crew listened as the pings subsided. They were hoping for the best.

*   *   *

The torpedo tracking the Archerfish had lost trail and begun its circular search pattern. It circled to the right as it slowly aimed toward the surface, its onboard computers listening before it again switched to active ping-mode. It was programmed to "think," to extrapolate the most probable current position of the target by considering its speed and last heading just before it lost contact. The last time it had contact, the Archerfish was headed for the surface. So, the leading edge of the torpedo's lateral stabilizers pitched slightly downward, sending the torpedo upward.

Rising one hundred fifty feet, the torpedo began another circle, pinging and listening. After completing one more circle it resumed its climb into another circular search pattern. A few moments later it received another echo, return ping. The torpedo's sophisticated logic was paying off. After a few more low frequency pings emanated from its blunt nose, it received return pings and straightened its course. It had reacquired the Archerfish. With engines revving, it accelerated to pursuit speed, refining its heading with each new ping.

*   *   *

Inside the sub the pings had grown louder, and faster, "Damn!" the captain cursed. "Ahead half speed! Get those countermeasures ready!"

In the torpedo room crew members quickly pushed torpedo-like devices with their sleeves into torpedo tubes one and two. Sharing the same sleek look with torpedoes, countermeasures have their own launch sleeves that fit within the torpedo tubes of the submarine. The sleeves provide a silent track for the countermeasures as they are propelled outward. Once the sleeves and countermeasures are installed, the torpedo tube is quietly filled with seawater. The outer door is then opened and the device is ready to swim out under its own battery powered counter-rotating props.

Koresh looked at his lieutenant commander, "Reigle, on half-speed mark, fire countermeasures."

"Yes Sir."

Reigle and the helmsman stared at the speed-dial. The stress on their faces intensified as the needle moved down toward the half-speed mark. The Archerfish slowed, settling to half-speed, and Reigle yelled, "Fire countermeasures!"

*   *   *

The props of the countermeasures engaged and began to propel the devices out their sleeves, forward and at a slightly down angle from the route of the Archerfish. Once cleared from the subs bulk, the countermeasures started broadcasting the noise frequencies of the Archerfish, the parent submarine. Its audio profile had been mapped and programmed into the countermeasures' computers. The countermeasures moved at the same speed as the Archerfish's half-speed, giving the incoming torpedo not one but three separate targets to choose. It could only follow one. The sub had just reduced its odds of being pursued by sixty-six percent.

Captain Koresh ordered the auxiliary systems of the sub turned back on. The ship began emitting the same noise signatures as the countermeasures. To broadcast simulated noise, the countermeasures trailed out a transponder eighty feet aft of their props. This mimicked the length of their parent, the Archerfish. Their sonar foot-print would look just like that of the Archerfish, and hopefully draw the torpedo away from the sub. It was their only hope at this point.

The torpedo continued to follow the submarine and the two countermeasures until one of the countermeasures broke hard to the left. But the torpedo's computer was not fooled. The torp stayed locked on the submarine and the second countermeasure diverging to the right, together, although at this point unable to distinguish between the two shapes. To the computer mind of the pursuing torpedo, both sub and secondary countermeasure appeared as one target. The torpedo closed the distance.

* * *

"Captain, torpedo in pursuit of us and our shadow countermeasure," reported Ears, his voice steadier. The tension eased. He had confidence in the proven success of countermeasures. He expected the torpedo to break heading with the sub at any moment.

"Heading five degrees Port!" the captain ordered. "Increase speed ten knots!

"Let's parallel that countermeasure. Stick with it boys."

Koresh concentrated on keeping the shadow countermeasure between the torpedo and his submarine. His hope was to keep the profile of the sub to a minimum. With the countermeasure now closer to the torpedo—and much louder than the sub—the countermeasure should register larger to the torpedo. Hopefully, the torp would take the bait and target the decoy. It was good doctrine and a good plan. If it worked.

* * *

Still pursuing both the countermeasure and the Archerfish, the torpedo switched to a faster ping rate, its rate of closure increasing. With closer proximity the torpedo picked up two distinct returns, causing it to slow and begin a snake search pattern, broadening its perspective to determine the larger target. The Doppler shift in frequency made by the sub as it completed its port turn gave away its larger size even though its sound signature was quieter than the countermeasure. Unfortunately for the Archerfish, the new ICE-X programming accentuated Doppler discernment. The torpedo was not fooled, and made its decision, heading directly toward the sub. Closing in, it switched to a faster ping rate and committed to attack speed.

* * *

"Shit." The captain's word seemed to hang in the red-glow of the bridge. The crew's faces shadowed with fear. As the increasing frequency of torpedo pings bounced off the hull, Koresh and his crew braced for the worst.

"Starboard turn, eighty degrees!" Koresh yelled, never giving up. "Full speed!"

The sub lunged right in response to the helmsman's hand on the throttle, the engines whining louder, slightly muffling the torpedo pings that continued to echo off its hull. The torpedo followed. Like passengers in a falling airliner, the crew cursed the time it would take to die.

The pings grew stronger, and the torpedo blip grew nearer the center symbol on the sonar operator's screen. Sweat poured off his forehead, dripping onto the scope and blurring the trajectory line of the approaching torpedo. Then suddenly, at 200 yards precisely, the blip turned and decelerated, just before the final strong ping echoed off the hull. The last few pings had traced a sweeping arc that faded out another 100 yards away from the Archerfish—the arc caused by the forward momentum of the slowing torpedo as it turned away.

Ears turned to the bridge crew, his eyes filled with disbelief, and said, weakly, "We've done it. The torpedo broke off. It must be heading for a countermeasure."

"Say again," the captain said quietly, not quite believing what he had just heard.

"Evasion successful, sir!" replied Ears, regaining his voice, and allowing his whole body to slump back into the chair, his back wet with perspiration. Evasion successful, he repeated to himself. Thank God.

CHAPTER 5

Ice Camp

Most Arctic camps are established and dedicated to scientific investigation: data gathering for both civilian and military uses, observation of native wildlife, and more recently tracking trends in climate change. These camps were often "joint ventures between academic and naval regimes," as described by documents at the Naval Oceans System Center, in San Diego, one of the agencies that ran the Arctic camps. In 1986, one camp did not fit such an esoteric description. Among its many distinctions that set it apart from other camps, this one was code-named. ICE-X '86 was located about half way between Prudhoe Bay Alaska and the North Pole, and, as it's code status implied, it had many secrets to keep.

The camp was run by Dr. Francos, a civilian who had previously managed many scientific ice camps, but none with such a large military presence. His main job was to keep the camp's infrastructure going. His second job---this one unwritten---was to ask as few questions as possible about the military part of ICE-X '86, such as what activities went on at the remote locations that ringed the camp. Each location was at least a hundred yards away, and—unbeknownst to him—at least twenty feet below the ice.

There are no roads to ICE-X '86, nor any permanent airstrips, primitive as they would have been in such a remote location. All materials and supplies were flown in by transport plane or helicopter, since transport boats would be stopped by the ice pack some 500 miles south. The camp was large enough to support seventy people at any one time. Many of the civilian scientific teams rotated in only long enough to carry out their experiments, gather data, and leave. It was up to Dr. Francos to manage and log the comings and goings of civilians. Captain Clifford Dredge was in charge of the military contingency.

Dredge was also in charge of those few civilians with a military job to do. Trinola's team fit that category, one that Dr. Francos was frustrated by, since he had no real authority over them. But it was one he accepted. The civilians with asterisks in front of their names were none of his business, he had been told.

Military officials were themselves a little antsy about this particular category: civilians with military clearance and military duties. The easiest point of entry for a foreign spy would be among civilian engineers, a possibility that had been emphasized during stateside briefings, but one that even Captain Dredge no longer seemed to consider. It just wasn't a priority to be suspicious and watchful of people that shared tight quarters and held specific duties that required years of training. Everyone had secret level clearance and a job to do. Not much was locked up, nor would it have been expected to be.

Most crewmembers slept in Quonset huts, six bunks to a hut. Others bunked next to their scientific equipment in different quarters. Most of Alex Trinola's team—including, Jack Boncare, Len Morini, Kent Richerson, Greg Bounds, and Gary Tercar—slept in the hut with a sign "NOSC" (Navel Ocean Systems Center) on the door. Rob O'Nerhy and Ross Spiry slept in the torp-staging Quonset hut where the torpedoes and equipment were stored and readied. (Their nights may have been less restful had the torpedoes been filled with several hundred pounds of high-explosive, instead of the radio equipment and weighted ballast.)

There were six individual senior sleeping quarters in camp. These were canvas-enclosed, steel-framed Quonset huts put down on framed and plywood floors for insulation. The huts were heated with kerosene stoves. Capt. Dredge's Quonset hut was smaller than most, but that just kept it a little warmer.

There were several other buildings—wood framed with plywood skin—that housed scientific instrumentation and communications, storage, an infirmary, and the Canteen. The Canteen was the social center where crewmembers gathered to eat and relax together. It was kept the warmest of all the buildings.

There was a rumor that some of the military guys—navy divers, probably—had a sauna in one of their huts, and some stories of beer parties with the female cooks. This brought to mind the North Pole tradition called the "100-degree club." Membership required participants going from the hottest inside environment into the coldest outside condition, in as little time—and clothing—manageable. A home-built sauna would fit perfectly into that tradition. The occasional empty beer cans at the dump gave it further credence.

At the perimeter of the camp were a half dozen outhouses, as well as several foot-tall enclosures with the overly-descriptive name of "urine boxes." These were open-top boxes, about four-foot square, that Dr. Francos required all the male camp members to use in order to monitor their hydration levels. Dehydration is a constant medical concern in this "cold-white-desert," where temperatures are low and humidity is zero. When colors in the boxes started turning dark yellow, the doctor encouraged more liquids. Lives depended on it, even though the running joke was that it would be easier to just urinate on the side of Dr. Francos' tent. "Less walking for you, doc," one nameless voice had called out from the back of the mess hall during the first briefing. Laughter exploded in approval to the suggestion.

Unperturbed, Dr. Francos took the comment in stride and reminded everyone that the urine boxes had two purposes: to monitor hydration levels and to mark the camp's territory from the Arctic foxes that would eventually discover the installation. The doc seemed delighted to reemphasize the point. "The urine boxes keep the foxes at bay, but more importantly, they remind you to drink plenty of water. Use lots of water inside you and very little ON you!"

That was the doctor's way of telling the crew members to wash sparingly and take only one shower a week, to minimize drying out the skin, a requirement which reminded the engineers at camp of their old college dorm days. Engineers, the doctor knew with appropriate irony, needed to be reminded TO wash.

The food at the camp was cooked by three female undergraduate students from Washington State University, for which they received a semester's credit. The only women in the camp, they slept in the back room of the Canteen hut, coincidentally the site of the only warm shower in the Arctic. The shower was a bug-spray-like system, a hand-pumped water vessel with a flexible hose and showerhead hung on the wall. The shower was off-limits to all other camp members, except for the occasional male kitchen helper. And the technician who was placed in the shower after falling through an ice hole while gathering salinity samples. Dr. Francos insisted he remain under the warm water until his body temperature had returned to normal. Seeing that, Kent once threatened to throw himself into an ice hole, just to get a hot shower, a threat that Dr. Francos knew wasn't serious.

But Kent was being serious.

CHAPTER 6
Keeping Score

In the communications hut at camp, Kent turned from his console toward Greg, "Wow, what a maneuver! That torpedo's just completed strategy D9. It detected countermeasures in the water, slowed down to distinguish targets, and then made a decision to follow the sub, until it finally shut down at turn-away. This is the first time I've actually witnessed strategy D9!"

"Greg, how long did it take you to come up with that program?"

Greg smiled, clearly proud of the test's success, "About three months. It's kind of complex—with all that nine-degree Doppler logic."

"Well I LOVE it when things work! That's fourteen for fourteen. They haven't beat our torpedoes yet!"

"I wonder if the subs know the score," Greg thought out loud, looking back at the monitors and tapping a pencil on the positional blip. "Do they know they are trying—and failing— to evade OUR torpedoes?" He paused, considering for the first time what it must be like inside a hunted sub. "OUR torpedoes or somebody else's?"

"They'll find out when they finally see the records," Kent replied. "I just hope they appreciate all our hard work," smiling.

"Don't expect them to buy us a round, Kent. If I were them I'd be pretty pissed...not to say that their pants aren't already...ha."

Kent turned to their silent partner, at the end of the table, with his own set of monitors. "I hope you are getting all this stuff recorded Spiry."

Spiry replied dully, "Yes. Everything."

Okay, that's two whole words you've said today, Kent noted to himself. He still wasn't clear why Spiry was on the mission, much less in the same room as he and Greg. Seemed like too much duplication to him.

Kent and Greg busied themselves shuffling papers, filing their notes into metal boxes on the floor of the heated hut. Their faces beamed with the delight of another successful day of tests, happy their torpedoes— or, more accurately, their programmings—continued to score against the subs. They took their time tidying up the communications hut, savoring the day's positive events.

Taking a final look around, Kent said, "Well, that should do it for today. Spiry, turn on the backup recorder and let's head for the Canteen."

"You two go ahead," Spiry replied. "I'll just finish here and catch up later."

Kent and Greg tucked themselves inside their parkas, and pushed open the door with their gloved hands. A harsh wind cut through the communications hut, but Spiry ignored it as he collected the separate tape recordings and checked them against a tally sheet. Glancing back at the now closed door, he waited for a good ten seconds, his head cocked for human sounds from the outside. Hearing none, he donned a pair of earphones with attached microphone and turned on a secondary communication panel. The panel hummed as it powered up. Spiry's face was framed against the light of the monitor as it gradually glowed to full brightness. Spiry glanced once more at the door, then turned back to the monitor. He figured he had about fifteen minutes before his absence would be noticed. He didn't waste time.

Trudging through the wind on their way to the Canteen Greg shouted to Kent, "Wonder what we're having for dinner. Steak and potatoes would be perfect!"

*   *   *

Diver Down

A mile north of the communications hut, the rest of Alex Trinola's team was helping in the recovery of torpedo number 14. A new hole had been dug close to the last known coordinates transmitted by the torpedo as it shut down. That location was triangulated between some of the many hydrophones the Seabees had lowered through the ice during camp set-up. The hydrophones made up the listening grid for Kent and Spiry's recorders.

Locations of spent torpedoes were usually triangulated accurately, and recovery holes dug pretty close to their final resting places. But this time things seemed different. Navy diver Daniels had been sent down to attach a recovery line onto torpedo 14. Trinola looked at his watch. It seemed to him that Daniels had been down for an unusually long time.

Trinola touched the shoulder of backup diver Michelson, who had been standing at the edge of the hole. Michelson gave three short tugs on the torpedo recovery line, and then waited for a tug in response. None came. As if heightening the sense of drama in the moment, the Arctic wind howled, causing the team members to lean against its blowing force. Michelson looked over at Trinola, then back at the hole. He tugged again. And waited. Nothing.

Len yelled above the wind, touching both men as he called out: "Pull him up." It was what the other two men had been thinking, but there were risks in such an action. The thin tether line could easily hang up on a stalactite, pin the diver against an ice ridge, or even sever itself on the sharp ice. "Wait!" shouted Trinola. "Maybe the diver or the torpedo recovery line is hung up on one of the hydrophone cables."

"Rob, get on the snowmobile, drive to the farthest hydrophone and cut its cable. I'll run to the closest one on the other side and do the same."

But Michelson wasn't waiting. Double-checking his mask, and blowing air through his mouthpiece, he dropped into the hole. Bobbing back to the surface, he lifted his mouthpiece. "I'll follow the recovery line. Hold on to it and wait for me to pull three times, then pull the line up."

Alex Trinola was the commanding officer at the site, but he wasn't about to argue with a trained Navy diver on what could be a rescue mission. Trinola nodded in agreement as he turned and hurried off toward the nearest hydrophone.

Michelson disappeared into the water. Len yanked off his right glove and grabbed the cable, wanting maximum sensitivity to the tug he hoped would be coming. He leaned back, pulling up the slack, maintaining a slight tension. As if in a time warp, minutes seemed like hours. Suddenly, Len stumbled backwards as the diver's tether lost tension. Jack grabbed Len from behind to keep him on his feet, watching as the line slacked onto the ice, limp, and unattached. Whatever had snagged the lines had been released, so Len and Jack started hauling it in, hand over hand, nodding at each other with relief and assurance.

Rob's snowmobile eased through the driving snow and came to a stop near the men hauling in the lines. "I guess you were right, Alex," he called out. "The diver must have circled around one of those hydrophone cables without realizing it."

"Yeah," Trinola replied, "and either his tether or the torpedo recovery line wrapped around the hydrophone on his way back. That's the problem with having so many lines in the water."

The water in the hole bubbled as two heads appeared, and hands holding two tethers reached up, handing the lines off to Trinola and his men. Both divers crawled onto the frozen surface, removing their masks before standing up and joining the others in pulling the heavy torpedo to the edge of the hole. "We've got this," Trinola yelled through the wind. "You two get on that snowmobile and back to camp, out of those wetsuits. And don't forget to be examined by the doctor."

Not moving from his spot, diver Daniels spoke directly to Trinola: "We've got to get rid of those thin tether lines. The torpedo recovery line is good enough." But Trinola shook his head. "Human life is more important," he shouted over the wind. "Plus, if we lose one of you guys for lack of a tether, we'll never hear the end of it," he added. "And ultimately, few missions are worth such compromise—not worth human sacrifice."

Michelson looked at Daniels and mouthed an okay in agreement with Trinola. He was just glad he and his friend had escaped with their lives.

"Now, like I said before, get on the snowmobile and head back," Trinola insisted, ending the conversation.

Complying without further comment, the two divers slipped off their rubber fins and stepped onto the vehicle. Rob turned the ignition and pulled away as Trinola called out his gratitude. "You guys did great!" he shouted at their disappearing backs. Turning toward the other two men, he repeated, unnecessarily, "They did great." He added to himself, 'you guys saved my ass, and my torpedo.'

On the snowmobile, both divers silently thought about what had just occurred. The recovery strategy needed to be reconsidered. By the time Daniels located the torpedo and Michelson found him, Daniels was almost out of oxygen. Halfway back to the surface, Michelson had to start sharing his air. He would write that in his report, he thought to himself. This is dangerous enough work without taking more chances than necessary...maybe triple air bottles were needed.

*   *   *

Who Knows What

In the communications hut, Ross Spiry completed typing in the data and transmitted it directly to Navy Secretary Lehman at the Pentagon. Then changing transmission frequencies, he reformatted the text and sent it off again. Looking around the hut one more time, he reset the dial back to its previous frequency, turned off the machines, stood, and grabbed his parka from the hook near the door. He braced against the expected wind as he stepped outside. Spiry was hungry, but instead of heading toward the Canteen, he took a ninety-degree detour.

Captain Clifford Dredge was standing over one of the urine boxes that surrounded the camp when he noticed Spiry walking toward the sleeping Quonsets. Dredge gave a half-second thought as to why Spiry was not headed for dinner. But too hungry to ponder any longer, he zipped up and headed for the Canteen. Once there, Dredge hung his parka on a hook, quickly loaded his tray with everything he saw, and walked over to join his Navy divers sitting together at a table.

Kent and Greg were already chowing down at an adjacent table. They sat with Gary, their contractor team member, who was on his second helping of steak. Predictably, the Canteen was filled with scientists, engineers, technicians—both civilian and military—sitting at tables, eating, and talking in scientific jargon. Kent and Greg exchanged a quiet glance at each other, silently noting the difference between their day and what the rest of the room had probably experienced. Dredge acknowledged their presence with a nod. He had at least learned about torp number 13 being successful against the Hawkbill. There was no question which group had the victory— smiles beamed on Kent and

Greg—although a little less excitement would have been welcomed by Dredge. The food calmed everyone as it satisfied their stomachs.

Their table was close enough to the divers that Kent and Greg couldn't help but overhear Captain Dredge in a debate with another officer. They seemed to be arguing over how much detail the three submarine skippers had been given about the tests, or "war games," as they kept describing them. It was no secret that Dredge thought he should be one of the skippers "down there," instead of being relegated to a base management position. Yes, he was in charge of the camp's military operations, but that command didn't have the panache of his old sub commands. And besides, he stewed to himself, most of the engineers and scientists didn't treat him with the deference he had come to expect. Sixteen years as a submarine skipper and he's stuck on the surface of some God-forsaken Arctic nowhere, just because the President wanted "new aggressive blood" for the fleet.

"It's not necessary for those skippers to know the details of these exercises!" Captain Dredge retorted, apparently to counter a previous statement that neither Greg nor Kent had heard. "In fact, the less they know the better."

Seated across from Dredge, Lieut. Cameron replied, with a little more firmness than he intended, "But Sir, knowing the torpedo turn-away distance would at least give those skippers a sense of security, not to mention relief to their crew."

"No, it's not necessary! In fact, the exercises are more true to life if those skippers DON'T know. In my experience, it's just second nature to take evasive maneuvers when you hear a damn torpedo coming atcha. A little detail like their turn-away distance is nothing compared to knowing all their sophisticated tactics. You just have to run, use countermeasures, ice formations, or whatever you have to outsmart them!"

Lieut. Cameron interrupted, incredulous at what he'd just heard, "Are you saying they weren't told?"

Captain Dredge recognized the shock in Cameron's voice, and turned to him. "Well," unsure of how much he should reveal to those at the table, "From what I hear about the aggressiveness of Secretary Lehman, they most likely weren't. Lehman probably wants the most realistic scenarios possible."

At that moment the door to the Canteen opened, letting in a blast of air that sent people lurching over to protect their plates from the cold. It had been a long day for most, even those confined indoors, and a hot meal was their reward. They wanted to keep it that way.

Trinola, Jack, Rob, and Len stamped into the Canteen, brushing off ice from each other's shoulders, their steamy breaths condensing at their words. Hanging up their parkas, they walked up to the table where Kent, Greg and Gary were seated.

"Wow, a little cold out there today, fellas," Trinola declared. "Glad to get back into some warmth."

"Yeah, I guess so, boss," Kent replied, a distracted look on his face, his eyes never leaving the adjacent table. "Hey, sit down here. I just heard something I don't like." Trinola and the others joined them around the table. Rob grabbed a roll off Kent's plate, something which Kent would have objected to had he noticed, but he had other things on his mind. Gesturing for the men to lean in over the table, he lowered his voice and said, "I just overheard Dredge saying that Lehman probably didn't tell the submarine skippers about these tests. They've been operating without knowledge of the turn-away distance of our torpedoes, or any detail at all about our exercises."

Trinola sat back up with a look of shock on his face. "What the hell?! They must be shitting in their pants."

"Or dying of a heart attack," Len offered.

"Setting aside for the moment the emotional duress we just put those crews under, what does that mean if one of our torpedoes misses the switch and hits a sub? All the blame will be on us!" Jack exclaimed.

Trinola continued, leaning back in over the table and lowering his voice. "Not being totally open about these exercises will just compound any problems. And, ultimately, MY head will roll!"

Anxiety started to take hold of Trinola, deep in his gut. He believed his career has been put in jeopardy—he might've been set up for anything going wrong—someone to blame. Was he a scapegoat for the navy even from the very beginning? All the worst possible scenarios started filling his mind as emotions took over his face.

Trinola turned toward Captain Dredge and, with a snarled look, pushed himself away from the table, and stood up, ready to confront him. But half way to the other table, the door burst open and Doctor Francos rushed inside. "There's a fire!"

To the instant attention of everybody in the room, Francos went on, "We need all you guys over to Captain Dredge's Quonset. No panic, but hurry!

"And Trinola, we may need your guys to transfer water on your snowmobiles.

"Let's go!"

Grabbing which ever parka was closest, the men ran out toward the burning hut. Some carried fire extinguishers, others shovels as flames encircled the hut twenty yards away. The fire had already eaten through the canvas walls, and the plywood flooring was heaving in spurts of combustion, feeding the growing fire and sending bright sparks into the illuminated night air. Black smoke gushed from the metal portion of the roof of the Quonset, and poured out every crack in its metal sheeting. More smoke billowed from around the chimney of the kerosene heater that protruded through the roof.

Peering through the conflagration, Len beckoned to Alex and Gary, noting that, strangely, the kerosene heater itself didn't seem to be on fire. They quickly ran around to the outside fuel feed and Len turned off the valve on the barrel that supplied kerosene into the hut. "That won't quiet the fire, but at least there won't be an explosion," Len yelled above the crackling flames. Alex and Gary then pushed the barrel off its pedestal and rolled it yards away just to make sure.

The floorboards raged with intense flames as portions of the thin metal skeleton began to melt. The structure twisted and slumped as the burning floor began to melt the ice below. The door and only window of the hut collapsed inward feeding the flames even more. The men moved away from the lost cause, dropping their fire extinguishers in frustration.

Rob pulled up on the snowmobile loaded with three fifty-gallon barrels of water. Hoses were quickly attached to the barrels and furious pumping began. The hut couldn't be saved, but the fire still had to be extinguished. Fire is an unpredictable thing, especially at a remote Arctic camp, and the men weren't taking chances with the remaining huts. Within minutes the fire was dampened, then extinguished. The water gradually formed an icy hump that would be even more visible in the morning light.

Coming out of a nearby hut, Spiry noticed the activity, and in no particular hurry to help, walked over to investigate. But the fire was already out and everyone was standing around the wreckage: a smoldering floor and wall next to where some of Captain Dredge's logs and other data were stored.

Dredge looked down at the wet, charred floor of his hut and grimaced, "Well, it doesn't look like there's too much damage," he said facetiously. "Hopefully we can repair it tomorrow. Ah... we'll have to sacrifice on sleeping accommodations for tonight."

He turned toward his navy divers for concurrence. They knew full well that meant giving up their hut for the night.

While Dredge talked over housing details with the divers, a few of Trinola's team noticed a case of beer under the burned out frame of a bunk. Alcohol was strictly prohibited at camp, and specifically prohibited by Captain Dredge himself. Those who noticed stared at each other in amazement, but said nothing. If anything, the presence of that Heineken confirmed in their minds Dredge's bias toward the privileges of his rank.

'What a hypocrite,' Trinola thought to himself as he picked up a blackened canister from the smoldering debris. "Captain, looks like some of the camps personnel logs are destroyed, but worse than that, it looks like the latest sonar tapes of the torpedo runs are fried, too."

"Shit! Looks like most of them," said Capt. Dredge, walking away from the divers and joining Trinola. He kicked at the ashes nearest him, connecting with something solid underneath. It was the remains of one of the logs, its black plastic cover melted onto a few still recognizable pages.

"We'll just have to rely on the separate tapes of the subs and torpedoes to recreate the data," said Trinola, looking down at the mess. It was then that he saw Spiry walk up behind them. Trinola had noticed that while most of the camp members had been running to the blaze, Spiry's response to the fire was more like a man walking his dog, in no particular hurry.

He gave Spiry a probing glance, hoping to get some indication of concern, but Spiry didn't look up. As always, Spiry seemed detached—in his own world.

Jack walked around from the back of the burned out hut, his face blackened by soot. He brushed ash from his gloves. "It looks like this fire was fueled by a leaky drain valve from the kerosene heater, and the floor was soaking up kerosene. I found an electric shaver cord hanging from an outlet on the wall and onto the floor—that could have started it."

"Yeah, that would do it," Rob agreed. "Let me check the circuit breaker."

In a few minutes the obvious had been confirmed. Trinola, Jack and Rob walked over to the blackened kerosene heater, just below the electrical box. Jack pried open the circuit breaker door with a screwdriver, revealing a row of melted switches, all but one of them in the open position. "Yep," Jack said, "This one's been tripped." Rob bent over and twisted the drain valve on the heater to the closed position. There was give, meaning it had not been closed all the way. Or that it had been opened slightly. The difference between the two conclusions was clear on the face of Trinola as he looked down at Jack: was this deliberate? Trinola shook his head, "I know what you might be thinking, Jack, but why would anybody want to destroy personnel records?"

"Don't forget, though," Rob said, "The sonar tapes of the successful torpedo runs were also stored in here."

Trinola nodded slowly as both men looked at him. He didn't want to think about the implications of what they were thinking. It just couldn't be sabotage, he insisted to himself. We're in the middle of nowhere, everyone's got top security clearance and Secretary Lehman had personally assured him the lid was tight on this one. But the more Trinola thought about it, the more his suspicions grew.

"It's a damn shame," a voice from behind them said. The three turned to see Spiry standing behind them, lighting a cigarette with an ungloved hand. "Somebody should be more careful next time."

Captain Dredge walked up to them, just in time to hear Spiry's words. Trinola was about to question where Spiry had been when the fire started. But Dredge interjected, "Yeah, an analyst like yourself would never have been so careless... I don't appreciate you accusing me of negligence."

As they all watched Spiry turn and walk slowly away, they heard Dr. Francos call out loudly, "Okay, listen up people. Since we're all here, this is probably a good time to update you on the status of the camp's condition. You know we've been here almost three weeks and everyone is working together beautifully—this damn fire notwithstanding—but one word of caution. It's taken ten days for the birds to find our camp.

You've probably seen them. It took another week for the arctic foxes to find us. They've been sniffing around our garbage for the last few days, but our urine boxes around our camp have been keeping them at bay. "Now, here's the warning. In a few more days, or even sooner, polar bears will know where we are. They're never far behind the foxes. But unlike the foxes, they want more than our garbage. They want US!

"From now on, be very alert, especially when you leave camp. Don't go out alone and always have someone with a rifle. It's April and mother polar bears are coming out of hibernation with cubs. They are very protective, hungry, and need to feed, so be very alert. Remember, we look like lunch to them."

Trinola watched Spiry walk back to his hut, not paying attention to the warnings Dr. Francos had just given.

Distracted at last from the smoldering ashes of Dredge's hut—and from the questions about its cause—Jack smiled at the mention of rifles. He had loved the firearms training before the mission and had turned out to be a decent shot. Len, on the other hand, feared shooting what he called "the elephant rifle" because it always gave him a bruise no matter how tight he held it against his shoulder. Bruise or no bruise, he told himself as Francos went on, up here on the Arctic ice, those rifles are our only defense against the polar bears. Even Len would shoot his riffle to avoid being eaten.

"Another thing," Dr. Francos went on, "We have heard from the weather bureau about the possibility of a quick-moving storm heading in our direction. Estimates are forty to fifty mile-an-hour winds, and if temperatures get down to minus eighty degrees we might have complete 'white out.'

"If that's the case, I don't want anyone outside. White out conditions mean disorientation and frostbite. Stow in some water and a little food in each of your huts, just in case.

"And one other thing," Francos added as something else occurred to him, "Tomorrow is Easter Sunday. Len Morini has offered to give a little message; 07:00 in the Canteen for those who want to attend. Len is taking some theology classes. It might be worth your time."

"God, it's cold out here! Let's get to the canteen." Shouted Dredge.

Just as Greg had envisioned, that night's dinner consisted of steak and baked potatoes. And even though it was rudely interrupted by the fire, dinner resumed and turned out to be one of the camp's best. It came with delicious salads, walnut dressing, three different types of vegetables, and elegant French sauces. The main course was served between minestrone soup with freshly baked sourdough bread. Two types of fruit pies were dessert. There were second and third helpings for everyone. Nobody said it, but each prayed that if another hut burned down it wouldn't be the Canteen.

Their bellies full, the camp's men headed off to a good night's rest. As instructed, they each carried a tin of water and some leftover bread, in case Dr. Franco's storm came in before dawn. The burned hut would have been the nightmare taken to bed had the great meal not completely changed the subject.

A few hours later, a little before midnight, a fox walked stealthily through the camp, foraging for garbage. Its nose travelled low over the snow, searching for scents. It stopped abruptly and raised its head, cocking it ears in the direction of one of the huts. Through the plastic windows—their panes streaked with beads of condensed moisture— unfamiliar sounds were audible to the animal. It turned and ran back into the darkness.

Inside the hut, Daniels turned up the volume on the cassette player, and then joined Michelson and a third navy diver in stripping down to their skivvies. A make-shift hot tub stood in the center of the hut, already occupied by Patricia and Sue, two of the women cooks. As the three men stepped down into the super-heated water, one of the women spoke up, "From what I've been told our submarines aren't doing so well against those smart torpedoes."

"Yeah, well it's probably not a fair fight," replied Daniels, lowering his shoulders into the water. "Trinola and his guys are shooting torps from the surface of the ice, taking our sub skippers by surprise. In a real fight our skippers would know where other subs were and have a clue where torpedoes were coming from."

Patricia thought a minute and asked, "Don't the skippers believe their subs can hide behind ice formations?"

"Certainly," Daniels quickly answered.

"Well, if that's the case, those skippers wouldn't know where enemy subs would be hiding anyway, or where torps would be coming from. It would be just like what Trinola is simulating, wouldn't it?"

Daniels composure stiffened, as if caught in a lie. With an accusing grimace he quickly added, "Yeah well, Trinola is just cunning enough to cut all the corners to make sure his torps catch all our subs off-guard."

Michelson snorted in disagreement. "Yeah, just like he was cunning enough to cut you loose and save your hide under the ice!"

The women looked at each other with questioning eyes, but Daniels lunged for one of them and said, "Here comes a torp now!" He mimicked torpedo pings just before submerging toward her. She moved, trying to avoid him but he wrestled her down until they both emerged with playful splashes.

"Quiet you guys," said the third diver. "We don't want to wake the whole camp."

"Yeah!" said Daniels, "Pass me another beer!"

CHAPTER 7

A Service of Sacrifice

The unauthorized hot tub was one end of the cultural spectrum in camp. At the other end was the strong religious commitments of many of the camp members. At an Easter service Len preached a message of Christ's sacrificial love, of a journey to the cross that led to the redemption of everyone. He said, "In like manner, we should be gracious, for we don't really know the significance of the good things we do. Our small sacrifices may someday change history. The rewards may be greater than we think. If Jesus was willing to hang on that cross and wash away our sins by his blood, then we should be willing to offer each other the least amount of favor." The head cook was so touched by his sermon that she offered Len a coveted space in the queue for a warm shower that same night.

Maybe the words "hang" and "wash" reminded her of the sprayer that hung on the backside of her kitchen wall. At any rate, she offered it, and Len happily accepted, and got the cleanest he had been since his arrival at the camp several weeks before. Len's whistling back to his hut alerted his tent mates that something was up, but they all guessed he was just filled with the Spirit. Maybe so, but "washed in the shower" was what he was really happy about.

Len's Easter Sunday message might have bought him a warm shower, but for some of the men it just stimulated a few heated arguments at dinner that night. Arguments about Jesus Christ's sacrifice and redemption for humanity turned toward the questionable need for religion and faith in general, and how several wars throughout history were spurred on by religious fervor. No one said it, but questions as to how all this ultimately related to what they were doing at the top of the world—and Reagan's policy of "Peace through Strength"—certainly entered their minds.

Later that night, Greg provoked Jack about religion instigating every war. "I can't think of a single war that wasn't started by religious zealots."

"What about World War II," Jack asked.

"Hitler used religious imagery when he talked about the Master Race and Germany's destiny. He invoked a holy crusade for German purity and the German church backed him up."

Jack didn't buy it. "I think that wars—ALL wars—are about economics. It's about the haves and have nots. Not to mention the windfall profits made by weapons manufacturers. Wars are ALWAYS big business to those guys! They just twist religion to agitate the people and promote their economic gain. Hopefully, what we're doing up here will put an end to all that nonsense!"

"Hey, what brought this on?" Trinola inquired as he sat down at the table between the two men. He had hoped to eat his meal in peace but he sensed he was going to get indigestion out of this interchange unless he cut it short. "Hey, I think you're both right." Once again trying to calm his own people and maintain group cohesion and civility, Trinola attempted to deflect the arguments. "Okay, new topic. Tomorrow is supposed to be warmer by at least a couple degrees. Anybody got an argument with that?"

As predicted, the next day added seven degrees Fahrenheit and seemed to relax everybody's spirits. The torpedo team got back to work cleaning up the staging equipment outside the torpedo Quonset hut. The sun felt so good Trinola's crew stripped off their parkas and flannel shirts down to their undershirts. They stacked the heavy equipment outside, ready for deployment. With the air temperatures hovering just below zero, it was an early spring day in the Arctic…, cold enough to make ice cubes, but sunny enough to lighten the clothes and even form a whistle while you worked.

In fact, the day seemed so warm the cooks announced the theme of that night's dinner would be Hawaiian hospitality, a well-established tradition in most ice camps, but one the torpedo team had never heard of.

The cooks decorated the Canteen with paper cutouts of palm trees, changed some of the light bulbs to yellow to mimic tropical sunshine, and put out centerpieces of pineapples, coconuts and bananas surrounded with paper leis and tropical flowers. Nobody bothered to ask where the pineapples came from, or on which chopper shipment, even though they had never seen pineapples served at camp before. Asking too many questions took up valuable eating time. Suffice it to say, that fruit was a real treat.

The dinner looked like the cooks had been preparing for months. And where they had been hiding the ingredients was anybody's guess, because it was simply spectacular. The meal consisted of roasted pork, fresh salmon with Hawaiian poi and a type of lomi lomi sauce. There was a fresh asparagus-based salsa with the zing of ginger and sharp onions. The pork had a peanut sauce, served with a side dish of cabbage chutney with scallions and mangoes. Side dishes of rice and something like potatoes were flavored with pineapple, papaya and banana.

The torpedo team stood in the serving line, stunned and almost speechless. They had never seen so much unique food in their lives and they kept looking at each other trying not to grin too much. They didn't want to seem too much like the new guys, particularly if the permanent members of the camp were used to eating like this, a fact that seemed to be confirmed when most of Dr. Francos' crew and some of the military guys walked in wearing brightly colored Hawaiian shirts. Nothing causes a double take like thick parkas coated in ice crystals being opened to reveal short sleeved shirts covered with palm trees. Some wore their navy dress white pants—truly looking Hawaiian. Most of the scientists were prepared, too. Trinola's team would have felt pretty awkward sitting there in usual everyday gear, were it not for the incredible food on their plates. The spectacular feast made them focus less on the dress of others and more on their forks and knives.

"I wish I had packed my own Hawaiian shirt for the trip," Rob smiled as he dug into a hunk of warm pork, "But nobody told me."

"Yeah too bad. We're all going golfing tomorrow and it would have been perfect," Kent replied. "You all brought your clubs, right?"

Every head at Trinola's table jerked up in surprise, then broke into laughter. Colorful shirts notwithstanding, a golf outing was definitely NOT going to happen.

*   *   *

While ice camp was partaking in their Hawaiian feast above, 100 feet below, the officers of the Hawkbill were having their usual dinner—not as savory as Polynesian delights, but very good compared to other military regiments. It was the second round of dinner, and the captain and most of the officers would soon be in their bunks. Lieutenant Commander Maple and a few other officers would be rotating into the night's watch, like everyone periodically did to make sure they stayed familiar with the entire crew.

The idea of day and night is quickly lost aboard a submarine. Without natural sun light and its daily cadence, one's internal clock becomes out of sync, actually speeding up without external cues to keep it in balance. Having dinner—breakfast and lunch—every 24 hours is one of the cues that is purposely maintained. Calendars, posters of 'morning' and 'daily' duties, 'afternoon' and 'nightly' movies, all help keep the subconscious conditioned to what would be normal living conditions, even in the midst of watch-changes and task shifts in the middle of the night.

Maple was just about to start one of those watch-changes when he turned to Captain Smith with an observation, "Captain, today I was thinking that every attack against us, and for that matter the attacks on the other two subs that we are aware of, have always occurred in daytime."

"Pugh!" Captain Smith spat out a gulp of water back into his glass. "What is going on with this water? It tastes SALTY! When was the last time the desalination system was cleaned?"

"I noticed that too Captain," Lieut. Comdr. Maple replied. "I'll have that checked right away. But what do you think of my observation—all those torpedoes were launched during daylight hours?"

"Huum," Captain Smith expulsed, after taking another sip of coffee and staring into Maple's eyes. He was experiencing something like a Déjà vu, or as if to say the same thing himself. "Come to think of it you're right. Every torpedo attack has been during the day—nothing at night. That's kind of interesting."

"Yes, I've even confirmed it with Clancy. I wanted to make sure before I said anything to you."

"Where is Clancy now?" Smith asked. "If he's not settled in for the night, bring him to my quarters in a few minutes."

"Yes Sir," Maple replied, as he left in search of the crewman.

In a few moments Clancy and Maple were in Captain Smith's quarters, trying to deduce why these tests were unique compared to other submarine war games—attacks and various operations going on at all hours of the day and night.

"Come to think of it, Captain, all torpedo attacks have come between the hours of 08:00 and 18:00," Clancy offered. "That's including those against the Archerfish and Ray, at least those I am aware of."

As if the three were drawing the same conclusion at the same time, Captain Smith blurted out the obvious, "Either those skippers have been given orders to attack at specific times, or there is another reason why attack times are linked to the surface sunlight."

Lieut. Comdr. Maple was quick to add, "Yes, maybe those torpedoes aren't coming from the subs after all. Maybe they are being launched from the surface ice pack! Don't ask me why, but maybe…"

"Maybe somebody wants to surprise us as to location, but at their daytime convenience," Smith interjected. "They surprise, but the surprise is being diminished by the limited time frame, wouldn't you say?"

"But the attacks are still a surprise, since most of them come from out of nowhere," Clancy said. "And that's still the problem, even though I think we—and the other subs—are able to evade most of the torps, so far."

"Or maybe the subs are launching the torpedoes, but they're delayed to come alive at a later time," Maple offered. "Does that make sense?"

"Well gentlemen we will probably ponder this in our dreams tonight," Smith said, wanting to conclude the discussion and get some rest. His eyes turned to the door, suggesting the two men take their leave. "That is, Clancy and I. You Lieutenant are taking the night watch, if I remember. Have a good night and oh, make sure you look into having the desalinization fixed. I want to taste fresh water in the morning."

*　　*　　*

Top of the World Living

In an Arctic camp drinking water is in ample supply. It's frozen, of course, but most people assume that seawater---even frozen seawater— is undrinkable, or that it needs sophisticated equipment to desalinize it. But the Arctic landscape is dotted with so-called "blue ice," which forms when seawater freezes so slowly that the salt precipitates out, leaving water so pristine it actually has a blue tint. It's drinkable and easily identifiable. Camp members use snowmobiles to drive out and hunt for the distinctive blue hue, usually found in outcroppings of ice rising up from the frozen field of white. Once found, the ice is chipped away with ice picks, the pieces then gathered for transport back to the Canteen. It is then melted down in large pots, and used for cooking, drinking, and washing. To some, it is the best water they have ever tasted.

Another little-known advantage of living in such an environment is that gaining weight is difficult, if not impossible. It requires so many calories to heat up the cold air breathed into the lungs, people have to take in extra calories to make up the difference. Any work—such as cutting holes in the ice to launch and retrieve torpedoes—is initially exhausting to the camp members until their bodies acclimate to the extra calorie demands and their appetites adjust accordingly. So, camp members eat large meals at every sitting to satisfy their hunger. Meals soon become the major motivating factor in accomplishing any work. Crews imagine the meals waiting for them back in the warm Canteen and they work harder and faster to get there.

The cooks always prepare four course meals plus desserts every day. And those desserts are sometimes topped off with candy bars, which are often pocketed for later consumption during the days' outings.

A notable Canteen event involved Patricia, one of the cooks, who made an announcement at breakfast that a whole box of candy bars had vanished from the pantry. "I have no idea who took them," she began, after getting the attention of the breakfast crowd by banging a wood spoon against the bottom of a fry pan, "But I think it is an unfair and selfish thing to do. You guys get all the food you can eat, and then some. But you want MORE?"

Seeing that all eyes were looking at her, she continued, more forcefully, "What, you walk out of here bloated with good food but you need a midnight snack in your pockets?!"

The room was silent, soldiers and scientists looked at each other and wondered who might have done the deed and why Patricia was so agitated. As crimes go, it would be a misdemeanor, but for the next few meals desserts did not include the coveted (and easily pocket-able) candy bars.

Jack, who was often seen at work sites pulling a candy bar from deep within his snowsuit, was the object of no little scrutiny; but, didn't reward any amateur sleuth with even a single incident of snacking on a Milky Way. Either he was laying low, or his candy bar habits were infrequent enough to absolve him of suspicion.

A few days later, Patricia came out of the kitchen and, again banging the spoon on the fry pan, announced that a partial box of candy bars had been returned: "Evidently the thief has had a change of heart, perhaps stirred on by Len's Easter message, or by just plain guilt."

The incident was typical of group dynamics in a close knit community. Whether intentional or not, everyone reaches a deeper level of openness and intimacy than what they experience stateside. All attempts of privacy breakdown—it's too hard to sustain. It is easier to be honest and open when sharing small spaces and extreme temperatures. The camp becomes the common denominator, revealing the complexity of human nature—greed, consequence, redemption and forgiveness. So it wouldn't be long until the thief came forward, to be forgiven by the cooking staff, poked fun of by the crew, and ultimately welcomed back into the small town that was Camp ICE-X.

A week later, to no one's surprise, Jack confessed to a few of us. Patricia had suspected him because he tended to often ask for an extra candy bar to take back to his hut. But she thought better of accusing him directly or publicly. Keeping the unity of the camp intact was always more important, especially since lately animosity seemed to be brewing between the torpedo guys and the military guys who were rooting for the submarines. The military crew stiffened with dour expressions whenever another successful torpedo run was reported. Captain Dredge in particular grumbled under his breath at each new revelation of success against "his subs." He continued to resent his land assignment and believed he would be doing a better job if he'd been skippering one of those subs himself. Plus, his peers on the subs "working blind"—not knowing how they were being tested—was a source of slow-boil infuriation to him, even though he said that didn't really matter.

*   *   *

Scenario of Tests So Far

Captain Dredge's level of infuriation was consistent with what was going on under the polar ice. Ice camp dynamics were one thing, but the even closer-knit community on board a submarine stressed out by torpedo threats was something completely different. Nothing can compare to the stress of silently hiding and waiting for the next swimming bomb— "racing balls out to kill you!" The food may be good on submarines but what good is that when tension-produced stomach acids prevent digestion?

When the skipper tells you, the helmsman, "Hide the submarine behind that huge underwater ice formation," and as you do that, a speeding bomb comes toward you from the opposite direction, with pings bouncing off your hull louder than a frying pan's clang that your grandmother made on the porch on new year's eve, what can you do then?! Shit in your pants?

No, you're too much of a professional for that. All you can do is hope and pray the next words out of the skipper's mouth will somehow save your ass! But how many times can a skipper come up with a new idea? There are just so many defensive ploys, especially when the details of what's really happening are missing. Scheduled naval operations are one thing, but when unspecified types of tests happen, and last so long, who can hold up under the pressure? Then there is always the threat the Russian navy may interrupt the tests. What's to keep them away?

"Forty degrees starboard. Up angle fifteen degrees!" The skipper commanded. He tried to mask the nervous sounds of his voice that the sweat on his brow betrayed.

"Skipper," yelled the sonar man, "That torpedo's still coming for us! It has passed the normal 300 yard turn-away. This can't be a test!"

"God help us," the skipper whispered to himself.

Just reaching the 200-yard range from the sub, the torpedo suddenly shut down, sending out its final pings, so loud they reverberated throughout the whole sub. The torpedo broke off its pursuit. The computer switched to its default homing signal and the rudders turned the torpedo back toward its launch location. Like a dog that had been passionately pursuing a passing car, it reached the end of its block and turned back. Back to the little hole in the ice and the equipment that would lift it out of the cold water and up onto a skid behind one of the snowmobiles. Until next time.

"IT BROKE OFF! It stopped!!" the sonar officer almost collapsed in his seat, exhausted from what seemed an hour of trying to evade this unseen and unrelenting threat. Did the sub's maneuvers shake off the torpedo?

"No more pings, Captain."

"Jesus!" blurted out the sub commander, relieving his tension. He loosened his grip on the chart table where he had been standing for the past several minutes. "That's the ump-teenth time this week. These MUST be some kind of weird tests. Get me command NOW!"

The second-in-command started to issue the order but hesitated, then regained his composure and corrected his captain. "Sir, we can't go to antennae depth here. There's a hundred feet of ice above us. We're fifty miles from the nearest clear ocean." The lieutenant didn't add that their orders were to run without contact with the outside world. The captain knew that, all too well.

"Forget it," retorted the captain. "You know I didn't mean that." Then under his breath: "Damn it, what in hell is going on here?!"

*   *   *

Entertainment to Competitive Conflict

Despite the frequent drama that Trinola's crew was causing below the frozen landscape, above the ice it was a different world, one that held time for relaxation and occasional R&R. To that end, Rob had brought along some VHS movies for entertainment at night, and the Canteen was the site of frequent screenings of Hollywood movies that weren't too old. Rob's taste tended toward the action genre, however, and the films didn't lend themselves to repeated viewing. A car chase loses its sense of suspense after about the third viewing. The cooks tried their best to add to the movie nights by setting out fresh popcorn and soft drinks. The salty popcorn and naturally dry air of the Arctic—especially inside a heated Quonset—made the imbibers even more thirsty than normal, causing a long line to the one bathroom in the place and a general frustration with the evening as a whole.

What changed the evening get-togethers for the better was when Rob revealed that, in addition to his videos, he'd also brought along a set of darts. Enthusiasm for the new sport was quick to catch on. Most of the military men and many of the engineers assumed they had a natural affinity for tossing pointy projectiles at a stationary target. How hard could it be? But reality soon set in as man after man saw his self-confidence waiver then collapse altogether at a game that requires an astuteness of skill not common to most.

Rob and Jack became the most competitive, bringing to the sport an unexpected comfort level and expertise. Rob developed a rigid and well-practiced technique, while Jack was more freestyle. He never stood in the same place twice, altering his approach and follow-through seemingly at random. Despite his apparent lack of system or technique, Jack started consistently beating Rob by just the slightest margin. Other camp members began to gather regularly when the two men faced off. Some wagering was heard to have been made, although none could be confirmed by Dr. Francos, who absolutely forbade gambling.

After one particularly painful close loss, Rob mumbled to no one in particular that he had actually won a couple of San Diego dart tournaments. Not the most sensitive sort, Jack retorted that he was legally blind in one eye.

"Damn!" said a shocked Rob. "How can I be losing to this one-eyed beginner?!" That question provoked unexpected self-doubt in Rob and his usual congenial composure soon turned into a markedly lowered self-esteem. With each game—and each close loss—Rob's depression grew. Trinola noticed almost immediately that this was a new wrinkle in the carefully balanced personal chemistry of his team. He noticed with alarm that these silly games were beginning to affect Rob's work.

The competition between Rob and Jack started showing up in the way they prepared the torpedoes for tests, in digging holes through the ice, and it seemed like in everything. Slowly, but predictably, in Trinola's mind, their competition would turn into antagonism. And it did.

One morning Trinolo's team awoke to Jack yelling that it was "freezing in this damn hut!" The vent on the top of the kerosene barrel that fed the heater inside the hut had been closed, and sometime during the night a vacuum had formed in the barrel. That caused the flame to go out and the temperature to drop dramatically. A man in deep sleep could literally freeze to death. But for a dream about his wife that luckily awoke Jack, he and his tent mates might have simply died before morning. Jack thanked his wife in a letter the very next day. Talk about fate, soul-mate rescue, or divine intervention. Who knows?

The maintenance of the kerosene barrels was typically carried out by a three-man team, selected on a rotation basis to refill the kerosene barrels throughout the camp. To no one's surprise, Jack immediately blamed that week's team for causing the accident that could have killed him. That team was composed of Rob, Spiry, and Daniels, one of the navy divers. While Jack didn't give a second thought to the silent Spiry, or Daniels, he immediately suspected Rob, for no other reason than retaliation for repeatedly beating Rob at darts.

"Maybe if you spent less time practicing darts, you could remember to monitor the kerosene heaters a little better," Jack suggested, under his breath, one day in line at breakfast.

"I don't have to practice to beat you, even with one eye closed," Rob retaliated.

"Yeah well, let me remind you that I only have one GOOD eye, and I still usually beat you!" Jack replied, with full smirk, as sporadic laughter broke out in the mess tent.

"That's enough," Trinola said, loudly, knowing he had to finally step in and staunch their emotions. Tensions between team members would inevitably lead to some kind of accident or otherwise compromise the project.

"Are you two going to keep this going until you screw something up, or kill each other?" Trinola cursed himself silently for not stepping in sooner. Was he getting tired? Why hadn't he acted upon his first inclinations—he knew his team's frailties. Enough second guessing himself, he thought. It was time to be the strong leader they all needed.

"Everything you guys say and do reflects on my test program, so put an end to it right now!"

After that Jack and Rob seemed to cool off, each realizing there was something bigger than both of them at stake. In the meantime, the rest of the team noted Trinola's frustration and avoided doing or saying anything around Jack or Rob that would provoke another argument.

A few days later, as Trinola sat alone in his hut, writing down notes from the day's tests, he looked over at the kerosene heater in the corner, remembering the problems it caused. He looked away, broadening his thoughts to the current status of his tests, and his own feelings about the camp. He admitted to himself that lately he'd started taking things personally and had become short-tempered with some people in camp.

The weeks of isolation and non-stop focus on the project was wearing on him. Everything was pissing him off. Was it really true the sub skippers had not been apprised of these tests beforehand? Why was Captain Dredge such a pain in the ass to work with? Some of the military, and especially Dredge, seem to be threatened by the capabilities of Trinola's torpedoes. Diver Daniels was becoming easily agitated and drawing attention to the faults of others. Was he trying to cover up his own inadequacies and frustrations? Secretary Lehman's assurance of Dredge being a support to the torpedo team had never materialized. And what about that suspicious fire that destroyed the sonar tapes..., and the kerosene-heater incident in his hut? Was one of the military guys deliberately trying to sabotage the success of the torpedoes? And lately, antagonism within his team?

What the hell, I'm just tired, Trinola reassured himself, pulling off his shirt and moving over to his bunk. Got to shake it off, and keep focused.

His mind began to wander. Have I been set up as a scapegoat right from the start, an expendable laboratory manager without proper academic authority, a fall-guy in a torpedo program that the submariners want to see fail anyway? Some of the civilian contractors— Gary Tercar, for one— would lose follow-up contracts if the tests were too successful. Where was he before the fire started? Kent said Gary was already eating in the Canteen before he and Greg walked in. But wait a minute! Contractors couldn't possibly stoop so low as to sabotage the tests, would they?

As he crawled into his sleeping bag, Trinola said a silent prayer for strength. He would need it.

Chapter 8
Nature's Perils

A few days after the fire most of the debris had been cleaned up. Offices and sleeping quarters had been shuffled to accommodate one less hut. The tests continued without a hitch, and Trinola's engineers were feeling a growing confidence that their theories—and their equipment—were working as planned. More torpedoes had been launched, performed as designed, and retrieved with no surprises. No failures of electronics, software, or engines, no lost divers, not even a bruised finger during retrieval of the cumbersome torpedoes. Trinola was pleased.

But, as any engineer could tell any other engineer, not every variable could be planned for. It was a Tuesday, and the second test of the day was starting. Team members shifted the launcher with a torpedo into position over the ice hole. Rob was handling the wench when he turned his head to check the aft end of the torpedo. It was swinging in an arch that brought its fragile fins close to one of the quadrupod's uprights. Out of the corner of his eye, through what limited vision his parka allowed, he saw movement. The human eye can detect motion before the brain can recognize objects. Unexpected movement in the Arctic usually meant one thing: BEAR.

Circling about 150 yards from the team, a lone polar bear padded slowly, periodically pausing to sniff the air from their direction. It continued its slow, silent walk in an elliptical line toward the men. "We've got company," Rob said, nodding toward the bear. As the other team members stopped their actions and looked up, the bear lifted slightly on its back legs. It sniffed the air again, not so much for the human scent—which it had already gotten—but for the smell of other predators with whom it might have to battle to claim its prey.

Rob steadied the swinging torpedo, and stepped around to the other side, putting it between him and the bear. The other team members shifted slowly to his side, stiffening in fear, as Jack reached for the rifle.

"Everybody up on the tool shed!" Trinola whispered loudly against the wind, not wanting to shout and cause the bear to charge prematurely. "Except for you, Jack. You stay down here with me, so you can get a level shot at the bear."

The nearby tool shed was an eight foot-high plywood box that housed everything needed for a torpedo launch and retrieval. A ladder was nailed to its side as were large straps that were used to attach the shed to a helicopter for hauling away. Both the straps and the ladder quickly filled with climbing feet and clawing hands as the men ascended to safety, a relative term considering an adult polar bear stands at nearly nine feet tall. As the men scrambled to the roof, some kept an eye on the bear. Others looked down at Jack as he pulled a gun from its carrying case. It was the only gun they had, and they hoped it worked.

Jack pulled back the bolt on the CZ-550 magnum, eyeballing a shell in the chamber, and pulled against the clip to make sure it was seated and ready. Extreme cold can freeze a clip out of alignment, jamming the next cartridge and rendering the weapon useless. Jack was a good shot, but no marksman. He might need all five of the clip's bullets to stop a 1,000-pound polar bear. And this one looked hungry.

The men on the roof of the shed had marginal safety compared to Alex and Jack on the ice. And that forced Jack to remember his survival training. What was it about killing bears? Oh yeah, he remembered, the only way to kill a polar bear is to fire right at his chest when he rears up. He recalled shaking his head in the classroom and looking around at his smiling colleagues when the trainer said that shots to the head of a polar bear just glance off. That couldn't be right, he remembered himself thinking. But he wouldn't want to be wrong now, he told himself. Better to trust in the training than take a distance head shot that would just rile up the animal. "We've got to wait until he gets real close," he whispered to Trinola, standing just behind him. Jack squeezed the safety back to the OFF position.

Resting the rifle on the top of the torpedo, Jack sited the animal, and waited. "Right," Trinola replied, remembering his own class, "You'll probably only get one good chance to kill him, one good shot."

Trinola turned away from Jack, and reached into his parka for the walkie-talkie. Keying the talk button, he opened the frequency and whispered, "Kent, do you read me?"

"Kent here," the voice came through the small speaker, which Trinola immediately turned down. The bear had their scent, and was moving in their direction, they didn't need to confirm their position for the bear by making noise.

"Get the hilo out here ASAP! There's a bear circling and it's hungry for our butts. We got a rifle, but I'd rather not use it. Kent, do you read?"

Rob, Len, Gary, and the two navy divers Mickelson and Daniels were on top of the shed. They had decided to lay face down on the roof, pointlessly lowering their profile to a predator that didn't need to see them to find them. Polar bears hunt downwind of their pray, relying on their sense of smell before using their weaker eyesight. The men on the roof knew this, of course; hell, any dog could find them up there, but they lay quietly nonetheless. Instincts for survival are not always logical.

A sudden wind nudged the torpedo, which started rocking enough to ruin Jack's gun hand. He grabbed Trinola's shoulder almost dragging Alex with him as he moved off a few yards to a snowmobile. Crouching behind it, Jack brought up the rifle again, this time across the snowmobile's seat. He sighted on the bear, which hastened its approach and continued in an indirect line toward the men.

"Just like one of our torpedoes," Jack whispered. "He's got acquisition for sure. I wonder if this is how those skippers feel? Maybe he'll break off at fifty yards," he smiled weakly and looked at Trinola for a reaction. But Trinola was distracted by his own task, waking up someone in the communications hut. "Kent, did you read me! Kent, we got a polar bear situation here!"

The small speaker crackled, "Sorry, Alex, had to confirm hilo available. The bird just took off and should be there shortly."

A football field is one hundred yards long, and anyone who's ever run its length or tried to kick a ball downfield can tell you it's a long way. But in the trackless white of the Arctic plain a hundred yards seems like a short city block, and the bear looked to be about a half-block away. At seventy yards the bear had straightened his meandering path to a direct angle of approach. He was walking straight toward them. His breath could be seen as he lowered his head and sped up his gait. Alex held the walkie-talkie at his side, holding down the mike key so as not to hear another broadcast from Kent. Trinola wanted silence, and he got it. Watching the bear close he suddenly realized how quiet the ice pack could be. There was no wind, no sound at all, except for the beating of his own heart, his pulse racing.

The bear started moving his head from side to side, and then stopped abruptly and lifted up his torso, standing to get a better view. Remembering the survival training, Trinola braced for the sound of the expected shot. But none came. He turned quickly to Jack, who stood, still. "Jack, what are you waiting for?!" The bear took some deep sniffs of air and snorted, seeming to have confirmed his prey. He lunged back down to all fours and broke into a trot toward Alex and Jack.

His trot opened into a run. Head down and nostrils flared, saliva drooled from his mouth in anticipation of food. Jack stepped out from behind the snowmobile. He hugged the rifle to his shoulder and fired. The sound filled the quiet void, causing the men on the roof to jerk up, involuntarily. The bear slowed his run, not sure of his next move.

Not waiting, Jack aimed and fired again. And again. The shots seemed to echo but then blended with a new sound. It was the rhythmic thumping of an approaching helicopter. Surveying the scene below, the pilot pivoted his aircraft toward the bear. The chopper flew past the animal, which stopped in its tracks and turned its head toward the strange noisy object. He reared up as if to get a better look. Again, the chopper passed over loudly, this time within ten feet of the bear's head.

As the helicopter circled around for another pass, the bear turned and sprinted away. The chopper followed, staying between the retreating bear and the men. The pilot wanted the bear to commit to its new direction and not change its mind. The hungry bear, in a fast run, disappeared from view. The bear might get its meal that day, the men thought, but it wouldn't be them.

Satisfied, the helicopter pilot pulled back on his controls and returned to the men now on the ground. The excitement was over. And so was the morning's test, Trinola decided.

Back at camp in the dining room, Jack poured himself a cup of coffee and looked at his fellow survivors around the table. "By the time the helicopter scared that bear away, I had an accident in my pants!"

"Was that before or after you froze and didn't shoot him when you SHOULD HAVE!?" Rob asked. Then with an unexpected smile on his face said, "And why is it the guy with only one good eye gets the gun? I say Jack gets to hold the bedpan from now on, and somebody else does the shootin'." The men roared in laughter at the good-hearted jest. "Yeah, if Jack shot darts as bad as he shot that CZ-550, I'd have a lot more money in my pocket right now."

"Say, that was fast thinking on your part, Alex—calling out that helicopter before we became lunch," noted Len in a reassuring tone.

Trinola, half-heartedly accepting the compliment, said, "Yeah, well we still lost the whole morning because of that mangy bear. As soon as we get the all-clear from the helo, we'll be getting back there. But this time, let's take more guys and more guns."

"And don't forget a bedpan for Jack," Rob called out, ducking a handful of sugar cubes that Jack tossed in his direction. And all of them missed.

*   *   *

Weather or Not

Several weeks of successful torpedo tests had gained Alex Trinola's team a day's rest. Jack, Kent, and Greg had volunteered for a water run and had picked an out-cropping of blue ice about six miles from camp. They had chipped off a considerable amount of ice and started loading it on a trailer attached to their snowmobile when the wind started picking up. Small amounts of ground ice, swirling up like dust devils, bit at their faces as they worked faster to load the ice. The sun soon became obscured by white clouds. And then the temperature started dropping.

As they loaded the last of the ice onto the sled they looked up to see Rob and Len pulling up on another snowmobile. Rob yelled out to them, through the wind, "Hey, if you guys didn't notice, there's an

73

Arctic storm coming in! And Francos wants everybody back at camp, pronto!"

"Yeah, okay, we're almost done here," Jack, called out. "Just a few more barrels of ice for the water we need today, and we'll be out of here."

As Rob and Len sped away, Len yelled back, "Better make it snappy! You do NOT want to get caught in white out."

By the time Rob and Len arrived at the ice camp, the Arctic storm was pounding the tents and Quonset huts, making each one shake hard against its stakes. The "ICE-X" flag and several communication antennas had already ripped away from sixty miles-per-hour gusts. Minutes later, temperatures dropped to minus forty degrees.

Trinola ran up just as the two were covering their snowmobile, struggling to control the tarp until the bungee cords could be snapped into place. Trinola got right in Rob's face to be heard through the wind, "Better make sure all our equipment is tied down! Get Len, Gary, and Ross to help you." Trinola hurried off to move his own gear that had been set outside his tent. Struggling with the door flap, he started tossing his stuff inside, cursing to himself about the storm. "Looks like we'll lose some days because of this. Damn it!" Standing up to his full height, a loose coil of ropes in his hand, he squinted into the distance against the pelting snow. He knew he had more people out there. Loudly, he swore at the wind: "And if Jack and the guys don't get back soon, we might lose them too!"

*   *   *

Unexpected Arctic storms get worse before they get better, and this one was no exception. As Jack, Kent, and Greg lashed the last of the ice barrels onto their sleds they could barely see each other, even just a few feet apart. Feeling their way back up the length of the three snowmobiles they boarded and were relieved when the engines fired up immediately. The engines had enough residual heat from the trip out to ward off the freezing of gas lines. Sharp temperature drops can cripple snowmobiles.

They pulled away from the blue ice site, now covered in white and almost indistinguishable from the rest of the landscape. They slowly picked up speed toward camp. But with barrels of ice on their snowmobiles and trailers, the progress was slow. Blizzard winds brought snow-dumping clouds that made the horizon disappear into a diffused white background. The handle bars of the snowmobiles became their only reference points to keep the drivers from complete vertigo. Kent and Greg could hardly see Jack's lead.

Jack turned and called out behind him, "Stay as close as you can!"

Greg yelled back, "We better lighten our loads. We'll never get back before the whole camp is closed in!"

"No way!" Jack screamed. "Keep going. We'll get there! And we're not going to show up empty handed. We got a precious payload here."

Jack knew that if this storm was as bad as he feared the camp would be snow-bound for days and the precious drinking water he and his comrades were carrying could mean the difference between life and death.

Jack looked down at his handle bars, struggling to see the compass. He reached down to clear the ice that had begun to crystallize on its face. Thank God Rob thought of taping a direction finder on this snowmobile, he thought to himself. Thank God.

The howl of the wind almost muffled the noise of the three groaning snowmobile engines. They were running slow and blind and getting dizzy with disorientation. With no horizon or ice out-croppings for reference, Jack was totally dependent on his compass, guessing at a southeast bearing back to camp. Kent and Greg struggled to stay on either side of him. When one or the other would briefly lose visual contact they would crane their heads forward to catch the sound of Jack's engine, then pull alongside again. They were cold and wet, and very scared.

With the temperature hitting minus sixty degrees the wind intensified, blowing snow and sleet from the northeast. As Kent used his forearm to brush away the icicles on his face he could no longer feel the wind's pressure on his nose.

Jack crabbed his bearing to the left trying to compensate for the forceful wind, a force so strong his snowmobile was almost becoming air born. There was no horizon and nothing to see but white. All he could do was stare at the compass, but the needle didn't seem to be moving anymore. He felt like throwing up.

Jack pounded on the face of the compass. Even with his blurred vision he could see the compass freezing. Frozen crystals of ethylene glycol had formed on the needle inside the compass. Temperatures had reached the limit of the antifreeze and the needle had stopped moving. Jack felt a wave of nausea growing in his gut. He HAD to hold it together, he almost screamed at himself.

A rise in the surface sent Jack's snowmobile up a few feet into the air. It came down hard, causing the compass needle to break loose, but it quickly froze again into a new position. There was no telling where he was headed now, or how long he had been misguided. Jack cursed loudly while he tried rubbing the compass with his gloved hand. If only he could warm it up, maybe it would give a true heading.

*   *   *

Back at camp, Trinola was getting anxious. He had gathered Rob, Len, and Gary inside the torpedo staging Quonset. The wind was howling outside as Trinola yelled to Rob, "I am getting worried about Jack and the guys. It's been a half hour since you told them to get back here and they're not back yet!

"And incidentally, where is Ross?"

"Last time I saw him," replied Rob, "was in the communications hut trying to get some last minute information out. All this wind has probably trapped him there."

"Well at least he's safe inside," Trinola said, hoping it was true. "I wish there was something we could do to help Jack. But I'm not going to risk our lives going to look for them. We just can't take that chance."

Len pondered a bit, applying his engineer's brain to the problem, and then offered, "What if we shot off some red flares. They might be close enough to camp to see them."

Brilliant, thought Trinola and he quickly agreed it was worth trying. "Let's get it done, and fast!"

Rob opened the survival locker and pulled out an armful of flares. "How many should we use?"

"All of them," Trinola yelled back as he flung open the door to the hut and exited with Len and Gary close at hand. "Bring them out!"

Rob loaded the first flare into the gun and fired it straight up over his head. Flares burn at about 400 degrees, hot enough to spontaneously ignite anything they fall back on. But flare safety was not Rob's concern at the moment, and the possibility of starting a fire in this wind and cold was almost a scientific impossibility.

Rob kept loading and firing as Len and Gary fed him flares. Red blotches glowed above the camp, shining down and illuminating the tents in a bright amber light. But the light diffused quickly in the windblown white out sky. Rob kept firing.

Miraculously, Kent and Greg's snowmobiles were still alongside Jack's, the men's faces bundled within their parkas against the burning wind. Only their goggles were showing. They may have been lost, but at least they were lost together. Jack's compass was a frozen clock face that gave no bearing and provided no direction. The simplest of direction finders had become useless. They didn't know where they were heading, except into white nothingness.

With panic barely contained in his brain, Jack began to pray for some assurance that he was headed in the right direction. As if in answer, he saw the red glow of the flares up ahead. A weak pink at first, barely a break in the endless white, the flares were not recognized by Jack. But then as if timed like the ping-rate of one of their torpedoes, another glow joined the first, and then another, and more!

"THERE!" he screamed to his companions. "Over THERE! FLARES!" Jack turned his snowmobile to the right, toward the last few red glows visible between the sheets of blowing sleet. Kent and Greg were quick to follow, also seeing the saving red lights in the sky. They steered toward the newly acquired direction. A new-found confidence gripped each man as he piloted his vehicle toward the fading light.

They were now heading almost seventy degrees from their previous track. Could this new bearing be right? Jack thought to himself. He kept going, hoping for more red glows. There weren't any more. Minutes past and there still weren't any signs of color in the sky.

Jack turned to make sure Kent and Greg were continuing to follow his lead. Then, suddenly, a grinding bump and the sound of splintering wood told Jack that he had crushed one of the urine boxes at the camp's perimeter. With immense relief, Jack smiled to himself that a pee box had never felt so good! Kent and Greg had to swerve to avoid the mishap and looked back to see Jack dismounting to clear a piece of wood from one of his snowmobile treads. Kent and Greg grinned at each other, thinking that a pee box, intended to check their hydration and protect from marauding foxes and bears, would come to save them in this unexpected way. They had found the camp. They'd made it back. They had survived!

A half hour later, their snowmobiles stowed and lashed to stakes in the ice, the men gathered in the Canteen for coffee and hot scones. Jack praised the guys for using flares to signal the camp's location. Kent and Greg thanked the team for using all the flares. Trinola insisted on their attention: "What in the hell took you guys so long. Don't you know you could get killed out there today?"

Jack, trying to avoid the truth of them getting lost in white out conditions, quickly answered, "Well, we just wanted to make sure we got all the water we might need. No telling how long we're going to be hunkered down here because of this storm."

Trinola accepted his excuse, since it seemed consistent with Jack's work ethic, to get the job done—at any cost.

"OK, but next time, don't be so heroic," Trinola said, "Water is not our priority."

"Unless you're thirsty," Kent quietly noted to himself, taking another sip of the biting hot coffee. It had never tasted so good. His head still covered in the hood of his parka, he gave another sigh of relief. Finishing his brew he walked out and headed to the doctor's tent. Later, Trinola would find out that Kent had suffered minor frostbite to his nose and ears. This prompted another lecture from Trinola on the team's cohesiveness and the importance of their mission.

"In this dangerous place, the safety of the team is paramount if the mission is to be completed," he said. "The wrong heroics will jeopardize our goal. Let's make sure our sacrifices are for the greater good."

The team listened attentively to Alex's words of caution. Kent was thankful for his ears still intact to collect Alex's words. Jack was thankful for running into that well-placed pee box at the camp's perimeter. Greg would later kid Jack, "Clever of you to save us from being lost—finding one of our camp sentries, a pee box we thought was just to monitor our well-being. Probably your strategy from the start, ha?—testing the integrity of what was monitoring our well-being up here all along."

Kent quickly concluded Greg's humorous analogy, "Sort of like what we're all doing here in the first place, right? You know, getting our torpedoes to find and test our subs that sentry the U.S." The joke might have been funny if not so true. The next torpedo launch after the storm cleared would bring new meaning to their good natured bantering.

CHAPTER 9

The Dream

"Sonofabitch! This storm just won't quit," Trinola yells to his teammates. He leans against the slung torpedo as the wind tries to rip it from the quadrupod. "This thing just keeps blowing like a bad dream, and there's no waking up!"

"We'll have to get out of here soon, before white out!"

As Len, Rob, and Gary struggle to hold the launcher upright against the wind, forceful gusts make it almost impossible to keep it steady. Trinola braces his shoulder against one of the quadrupod's legs. Fears of frostbite start consuming his thoughts. He has to protect his crew, even at risk to the mission. They've done well with the weather cooperating, but not now. He understood Command's insistence for more tests—and the engineer in him knew the more data the better—but he feared the data might come at the cost of lives. His team was committed and, he knows now, brave. But he didn't want them to be martyrs to research that simply confirm what they already know: The program works. The software and hardware work. They've proved it time and again. The subs can't hide from the torpedoes. So why take unnecessary risks with the lives of his team?

"Keep that thing steady!" Alex yells, shaking off his thoughts, coming back to the present. "Kent, you got the recorder systems going?"

"Kent, do you read?! I'm about to pull the lanyard on this baby!"

Kent's voice cuts through the storm, "Recorders running. Com-hut ready!"

Alex curses at the lag time in communication with the base. It always takes an extra second to hear back and it's a long second that gives Trinola constant doubts about the link. He shouts out to the team, "Steady guys!"

Struggling with his end of the quadrupod, his boots having long ago lost their traction in the blowing storm, Len shouts back, "God help us! Maybe we should hold off till this wind subsides. Either that or the hell with it and get out of this storm while we have a chance!"

"I don't know if I can hold this much longer," Rob yells out, struggling to brace his left foot against the snow. Moments before he had slipped and stepped part way into the icy water, drenching his left boot which was now frozen solid. He was beginning to lose feeling in his foot.

Alex yells back, "Come on guys! Enough discouragement shit. We've got to do this right now!"

As if offering a counter argument, a strong gust of wind shakes the quadrupod, which snaps out of Len's grasp, shoving into his body and forcing him to the ice. Without hesitation, Jack runs over to help steady the pod and launcher. His bulk, muscles, and a few curse words aid in stabilizing the quadrupod. The torpedo launcher steadies and comes back into balance.

The moment has arrived, and Trinola doesn't miss it. He pulls the lanyard and the torpedo plunges deep through the ice hole, its engine starting automatically. The torpedo's counter-rotating props spool up, churning and splashing the icy water up at the crew. The water closes behind the torpedo, as if it was never there.

"Good, another torpedo away!" Trinola exclaims, "Now let's get in the tool shed, out of this cold wind." 'And let's see what those subs can do against this one,' he mutters to himself before turning his attention to the more immediate task: firing up the kerosene heater.

With the torpedo now away, the guys let go of the pod and launcher. They follow Trinola toward the shed, not noticing that the force of the wind carries both devices into the ice hole, where they sink immediately. They hurry to take cover in the four-by-eight foot plywood tool shed, about twenty feet from the ice hole.

Stepping into the shed, Alex turns back to the door and yells into his headset, "Kent, I hope that torpedo finds a sub real soon so we can get out of here!

"On second thought, forget the torpedo, Kent. Maybe you should send out the helicopter to pick us up now, before the weather closes in. We might have to wait for tomorrow to recover that torpedo, but it's better than freezing our butts off!"

Kent in the communication hut receives Alex's broken message, and replies, "Roger that. I'll send the helo right now! One lost torpedo won't be that bad."

Alex didn't reply, he was tired of yelling into his radio. In the sudden relative quiet of the hut he had lost all desire to talk to base, only to himself. 'As long as the torpedo acquires a sub I won't mind losing one. Our lives are more important.'

The storm outside the hut was getting worse. It shook the thin walls with what seemed a malicious effort to shake out the men, who were now safe, but very cold. Below the raging winds of sleet were the calm, dark waters of a different world. And in that world, a torpedo had just acquired another submarine and began its pursuit.

*   *   *

Against the dim light of the submarine's bridge, the captain walks to his chart table. He peers at the lines of contour that purported an accurate representation of a world that, in reality, could never be charted or fully known. A frown comes across his face, the yellow glow of the bridge seeming to deepen the furrows in his brow. Captain Alex Trinola is not pleased at his situation. And for good reason.

"Torpedo pings! Starboard bow forty degrees, Captain!"

Trinola looks toward his sonar man and nods. Trinola sighs with the recognition of another attack, another test, another journey to the edge of fear. Lieutenant Rob O'Nerhy retorts, "This can't be happening again, sailor! No way. Check your instruments!"

But O'Nerhy knows it is pointless to doubt, and he turns to Trinola, "What are we going to do this time, Captain? Sir, what the HELL ARE WE GOING TO DO!!?"

Trinola strokes his scruffy beard that seems to have grown in an instant, throws his skipper's cap onto the table and turns, angrily, to his lieutenant.

"Where's your faith, man?! We've broken trail three times now and you doubt we can do it again against this torpedo? Those things can't track us when we get behind the right ice forms and…."

Just then sonar man, Gary Tercar, shouts, "More pings Captain." The pings grown louder, but the crew cover their eyes instead of their ears. The pings have changed to flashes of red light, intense and blinding. Sonar man Tercar again yells, "More pings, I mean flashes Captain, but I'm not sure it's found us yet." Torpedo seems to be circling again, still searching. Shouldn't we be hiding somewhere?"

"Who's the Captain here?" Trinola yells back. "I make the decisions on this sub!"

The sub moves sharply left, causing the captain and Lieutenant O'Nerhy to reach for the table to steady themselves. Len Morini is at the helm and as the sub comes around to level he rotates the wheel slowly back toward the right. He is staring at his speed and bearing gauges and mumbling to himself, "Let's see, where were those big icicles? Starboard? Or port?"

Captain Trinola, still gripping the table to keep his balance on the yawing sub, can't believe his eyes. "Yeoman Morini, what the hell are you doing? Keep her steady as she goes!"

"Captain, we've got to get ice cover before that torpedo sees us," Morini replies, "Or we're dead."

Morini again rotates the wheel, while narrating his own movements, "Right rudder thirty degrees. That's an order, sailor. Left rudder twenty degrees. Right rudder twenty-five degrees. What a nightmare. Have to find that ice cover. Have to find that ice cover. That's an order!"

O'Nerhy runs over and grabs the wheel, trying to turn the sub to a reasonable heading, and yells, "Don't worry, we don't need any ice cover to hide. Captain Trinola is going to launch his own torpedoes to destroy the one after us!"

What is happening to my crew? Trinola asks himself, disbelieving his own ears. What has gotten into O'Nerhy? Where has that belligerence come from?

Over the com-speaker, a voice crackles into the control room, "Torpedo-man Boncare, Sir. Torpedoes one and two ready for launch at your command."

Trinola grabs the com mike and shouts back, "Who said anything about launching torpedoes? Is everybody crazy?"

Trinola turns back to the sonar man, fear gathering on his face, "Tercar, anymore pings? You know where that torpedo is?"

"Yes Sir. Its pings are on second base and it is going on to third. Two outs and the ball's flying to left field. Runner on third is heading home! But here is a good tune, right here."

A rock song blasts through Tercar's earphones, filling the helm with the sound of screaming guitars as he nods his head to the beat. Tercar is completely lost in the musical mutiny.

As Trinola looks around in shock, his crew members start yelling at each other. O'Nerhy and Morini are fighting for control over the wheel as Boncare's voice again comes over the loudspeaker threatening to launch torpedoes. Against the growing pings of the unseen torpedo, Tercar sings to the music.

*　　　*　　　*

On the surface of the ice, a fierce wind rips the ICE-X pennant flag from its post and it flies away into the darkness. The wind has no sound. There is only silent, sun-lit yellow sleet that flies into blinding white nothingness.

Trinola hears his heart beating in triple cadence with his panting breath, matching the punctuating rhythm of the torpedo pings. His senses burn with hypersensitivity. His skin seems on fire.

His surroundings are suddenly a disorienting white vacuum, then the warmth of emanating fire opens the pores of his face. He breathes in its heat, recoiling at the sudden change of temperature.

The taste of a steak has come to his mouth, and he chews with pleasure. The taste is overwhelming in its salty texture, but when he looks down he sees no table, no plate, no fork or knife. He lifts his hands to his face, but they do not appear. His focus adjusts to the near distance and he sees the table, finally, but with only a torpedo stretched out on white linen. The yellow light from the room gives the weapon an otherworldly glow. The torpedo is broken in two, between its fuel tank and engine compartments. Its Otto fuel puddles at the break like blood, soaking the table and spreading to the steak that has now come into focus.

The delicious taste of his steak changes from well-cooked flesh to the thick stench of fuel oil. Trinola's chest aches and his brain begins to throb as the fuel surges through his body. His heart beats faster, his pulse racing, and nausea surges up from his mid-section.

*   *   *

A confusion of throbbing pain gives way to a powerful sense of conflict as Alex Trinola sees himself playing each role of his team. He is first trying to launch a torpedo in the midst of the storm and then trying to order evasive maneuvers in the control room of the sub.

"What a storm!" He yells, to no one. "This thing just keeps coming. We'll have to get out of here soon; before we're trapped in whiteout!"

Gagging from the yellow fuel dripping from his lips he turns toward his men holding the quadrupod, "Launch another torpedo through the ice pack, the storm is getting worse. You'll get frostbite if you don't get to cover soon.

"Keep that thing steady! Kent, you got the recorder systems going?! I'm about to pull the lanyard on this baby!"

Through the wind of the storm a muffled voice comes through "Recorders running, Com-hut ready!"

Alex shouts, "Steady!" and turns to Len, who has taken on the form of Trinola, and yells back, "God help us! Maybe we should hold off till this wind subsides, and get out of this storm."

Voices, unrecognizable, cut through the storm from all directions, surrounding Trinola as he struggles with the lanyard line.

"I don't know if I can hold this much longer."

"Come on! Enough of your shit. I gotta do this right now!"

A strong gust shakes the quadrupod as Alex, now in the form of a muscled Jack, runs over to help steady the pod and launcher. Cursing and moving with superhuman strength, he stabilizes the entire assembly, moving the other crewmembers as if they were part of the device.

Alex pulls the lanyard and the torpedo plunges through the ice hole. Its engine starts instantly and propels it deep into icy blue waters.

Unrecognizable voices again surround Trinola.

"Good... another torpedo away!"

"Let's see what those subs can do against this one!"

Alex moves toward the tool shed and yells into his headset, "Kent, I hope that torpedo finds a sub real soon so we can get out of here!"

Then, calmly and slowly Trinola turns back and looks at the

horizontally blowing sleet that now obscures his men. There is silence. The sleet still blows across the scene, separating Trinola from his men, but there is no sound. A warmth begins to spread over Trinola as he pulls back the hood of his parka and brings the microphone to his lips. In a whisper he says, "In fact, Kent, maybe you should send out the helicopter to pick us up. No worries about recovering this torpedo."

A voice responds from the communications hut, but the voice is that of Alex, who calmly replies, "Sounds good, my friend. I'll send the helo right out. One sacrificed torpedo won't be that bad."

Alex smiles as the wind continues to whip silently in front of him and, one by one, sweeps his crew into the icy waters, where they immediately sink from view. He speaks into the mike: "Yeah, I won't mind losing a torpedo, especially if it sinks an American sub."

*   *   *

Aboard the submarine, the yellow glow of the bridge again gives a jaundiced tinge to the form of Captain Alex Trinola, deepening the lines of fear in his face, when he hears:

"Torpedo pings—Starboard bow forty degrees, Captain!"

Now in the role of Lieutenant Alex Trinola, Alex acknowledges, his voice rising, "Oh my God! This can't be happening again! What are we going to do this time, Captain?"

Captain Alex Trinola strokes his now long beard, tosses off his skipper's cap, and confronts Lieutenant Trinola's fear.

"At what point have you lost your cool. We've broken trail three times now and you doubt we can do it again against this torpedo?

"Where's your faith, man?"

Alex's attention is distracted by sonar man Trinola, who shouts, "More pings Captain." The pings grown louder, but everyone begins to cover their eyes instead of their ears. The pings have changed to blinding pulses of intense red flashes of light. Sonar man Trinola again yells, "More pings, I mean flashes Captain, but I'm not sure the torpedo has found us yet. Seems to be circling again, circling again, circling again.

"Shouldn't we be seeking some cover somewhere? Sir?"

"Damn!" yells Capt. Trinola. "Who's the Captain here?"

Helmsman Trinola turns the wheel to the right, then back to the left, mumbling to himself, "Let's see, where are those icicles? Starboard? Or port?"

Captain Trinola can't believe what he is seeing. What is going on here.

"Yeoman Trinola, what are you doing? Keep her steady as she goes!"

"But Captain, we got to get ice cover before that torpedo sees us, or we're dead," Yeoman Trinola yells back at himself.

Rotating the wheel, he repeats his commands: "Right rudder thirty degrees. Left rudder twenty degrees. Right rudder twenty-five degrees. What a nightmare. Have to find that ice cover. Have to find ice cover. That's an order!"

Lieutenant Trinola runs over and grabs the wheel, trying to turn the sub to a reasonable heading. "Don't worry, we don't need any ice cover. We are going to launch our own torpedoes to destroy the one after us!"

The com-speaker barks a static voice: "Torpedo man Trinola, Sir. Torpedoes one and two ready for launch at your command."

Capt. Trinola thinks to himself, Christ! Who is in authority here? We're not allowed to be launch torpedoes, are we? We have strict orders. Am I crazy?

He yells out to the sonar man, a yellow ghost of himself, "Sonar man Trinola, hear anymore pings? You know where that torpedo is?"

"Yes, Sir, its pings are on second base and it is going to third," sonar man Trinola says, this time in a sing-song cadence. "Pings on second, going to third, with two outs and the ball's flying to left field. Runner on third is heading home! Runner on third is heading home."

He again starts nodding his head to the rhythm of some rock tunes now filling the helm, repeating the sounds again.

Alex looks around, seeing himself in everyone, everyone in a yellow fairytale. He hears himself yelling and fighting for control over the wheel, threatening to launch torpedoes, and now singing to rock music.

This can't be real. How had he become this self-doubting, indecisive leader, torn between his own authority and the demands of the mission.

The sub shakes with a wooshing sound as a torpedo is pushed out of its tube and into the icy waters. Then another. They both buzz away, pinging toward the approaching torpedo.

Trinola yells out, "Who did that?"

"I did!" he answers back to himself, "Through my own authority, and I'll take the consequences! I give the orders here!"

*   *   *

On the surface a different confusion reigns, as strong winds rip the ICE-X flag from its pole in the center of camp. But there is silence. No sound from the sun-lit yellow sleet that flies into blinding white nothingness.

Under the ice pack, Alex listens to his heart beating in triple cadence with his panting breath.

*   *   *

Sonar man Trinola yells at Captain Trinola, "You've done it now. Our torpedoes are converging on a large ice form. They've lost the target and that nemesis torpedo is still heading right for us!

"You have sacrificed everything.

"The mission is lost.

"We'll be dead in … Four… Three… Two… One…"

A sudden explosion shakes the sub. The torpedo has broken itself across the bow of the submarine with a force that will send both to a deep watery grave. All is lost.

*   *   *

Surrounded by a dizzy white vacuum, Alex feels the warmth of an emanating fire that opens the pores of his face. He breathes in its heat and calming temperature.

His steak tastes delicious as he looks down and sees the table, his plate, his knife and fork. But where are his hands? He cannot see his hands?! The hands that had gripped the chart table, that had turned the control wheel, that had launched the torpedo, that had….

The door to the hut cracked open loudly as Len stepped over the threshold, a swirl of cold air reaching in to fill the small space. "Hey Alex," Len shouted, "Enough of a nap! You're late for lunch.

"The storm has finally passed!" He added, with obvious relief.

Alex woke with a start and turned his head toward a smiling Len.

And then Alex looked down at his hands. Both of them.

CHAPTER 10

Torpedo Tests with a Twist

The stormy, white out conditions on the surface of the Arctic ice pack have no effect on the calm and quiet underwater world below. It's as if two worlds, each alien to the other, exist side by side. The world above was a swirling din, a sub-freezing windstorm. In the silent world below, the USS Archerfish slowly motored in calm waters, maneuvering in a smooth ballet of movement between large stalactite ice formations. Inside the sub the quiet, steady hum of twin turbine engines provided a soothing soundtrack for the crew, the backdrop to the sailors' every move.

*   *   *

"Captain," the sonar man broke through the quiet of the bridge, "I got a definite acoustic profile. It's the Hawkbill 666 at about three thousand yards, forty degrees off our port bow."

Captain Koresh nodded toward Ears, the sonar man, then turned back to his helmsman at the wheel, "Good. Slow to an eighth; silent running status. We don't want those 'devil-ship' boys to see us. It's probably their turn to launch a torpedo at us, considering the Ray was most likely the last boat to target us."

Dropping his pen loudly on the chart table, the captain mused out loud, "I don't know why we're the only boat playing the pigeon in all these tests, why our orders don't allow us offensive launches like the other boats.

"But let's find some more giant ice forms and lay dormant awhile."

The helmsman of the Archerfish levered down the sub to one-eighth speed and the crewmen all shifted forward reflexively. As the craft slowed, the red lights of silent running seemed to highlight the increase in temperature within the hull of the Archerfish. Silent running requires turning off all auxiliary power systems, including the forced-air ventilation system. That means after awhile the crew begins to sweat, the perspiration adding to an already humid atmosphere, and stressing the crew even further. There is nothing like the sweat of a man to remind him of the unique mental tension of working in a closed steel container. Tapped below the surface, cut off from its life-giving air, his perspiration condenses on the surfaces that confine him. A submarine's innate vulnerability is never far from the minds of its sailors. A sub in silent running mode all the more so.

*   *   *

The green running lights of the Hawkbill's helm mirrored the 'go-n-do' mood of a crew that, in this particular moment, was confident. It was not war-time, and any unexpected intrusions would probably be from friendly craft nearby. Capt. Smith spoke easily, to no one in particular, "So far a pretty quiet day."

Looking up from his scope and stretching his arms above his head, sonar man Grahams replied, "Yeah, so far I have the positions of the Ray and Archerfish. That is, their last positions, since both are now cruising behind some ice blocks."

"Any bets on who will launch the next attack?" the captain asked, rhetorically.

Helmsman Clancy piped up, grinning, "My money's on Captain Koresh and the Archerfish."

Grahams added, "Could be. They've been pretty quiet lately."

"Yeah well, keep your ears open," Capt. Smith instructed, suddenly serious. "We don't want this hide-n-seek game to get the best of us. I know it's been going on for days, but let's not get complacent. Stay vigilant." Such words from the captain typically encouraged his crew and offered the decisive leadership that made Captain Smith the person everyone respected. Smith loved his career and felt it an honor to be on one of the "important submarines chosen for Arctic duty in these perilous times of Cold War." Those feelings trickled down and compelled his crew.

*   *   *

Morning of New Motives

It was morning on the surface and the winds were finally subsiding as Trinola and his torpedo launch-team loaded their equipment on snowmobiles and headed out to a distant location. Clear skies intensified the brightness of the sun, so everyone had applied 50 SPF sun-block on their faces and looked at the terrain from behind extra dark Ray Ban sunglasses.

Lashing the last of his equipment onto the back of a snowmobile, Jack Boncare said, a little too loudly, "I can't wait to get out there. We lost three whole days because of that damn storm. I hope that doesn't compromise our final few tests."

"Don't worry about it," Trinola replied, stepping high onto his snowmobile and settling in to the seat. "That break probably heightened the anxiety of the next shot for the submariners. They won't be ready for the next shot, which will test their reflexes, if nothing else. As far as the test program is concerned, the storm may have been a blessing in disguise."

"I hope you're right," said Gary Tercar. "We've had enough things go wrong."

Rob O'Nerhy turned toward Tercar, who was standing behind his sled, "What do you mean? Just because of a storm and those guys got lost on their way from getting water... doesn't mean something else will go wrong, does it?

Jack offered, "Well, you know what they say about things happening in threes."

Annoyed, Len chimed in with a tinge of anger in his voice, "Yeah, we know all about that superstitious nonsense! We need a little more faith."

"Don't worry. It will all work out for the best," Trinola found himself saying with a new sense of calm and confidence. His mind flashed back to those words of his wife when he told her of his apprehension of being set up as a fall guy—a fall guy for the Navy's project if anything went wrong with the torpedo tests and submarines were damaged. She was always so level headed, probably a defense mechanism she honed raising two sons just as excitable as their father. Thinking of her always calmed Trinola and brought him back to practicality. He smiled at the thought of her. Suddenly, he couldn't wait to get home, back to her and the boys.

With a couple of deep breaths to change his composure, Trinola expelled the words of the intrepid leader he was, the words he most of all needed to hear: "Let's just get out there and do our job." He waved a hand forward and the snowmobiles moved off in a tight single file. The storm of the past week had taught them to stay in each others' tracks and line of sight, regardless of the weather. Even on a clear day good habits proved the team was focused.

Below them, unseen and a mile back, the black hull of the USS Hawkbill moved quietly through erratic figures of ice, keeping an almost identical pace with the snowmobiles above. Then the Hawkbill turned ninety degrees and started to slow to one-eighth speed.

Trinola's team arrived at their location a half hour later. They quickly set to the task of cutting a large rectangular hole through the ice pack. While the team removed the ice from what looked like a very deep hole, Trinola summoned Kent through his headset, "Hole almost ready for Torpedo number 20. Kent do you read?"

Kent was just about to reply when the Hawkbill scraped against one of the hydrophones suspended ninety feet below the ice pack. To the crew of the Hawkbill it sounded like they had grazed a stalactite ice form, a little too close to the hull. But through Kent's headphones in the communications hut, it was a loud rasp of metal against metal.

"Shit!" Kent yelled to himself, throwing off his earphones to protect his ears from the torment. Then keying his mike he yelled out, "Alex, the Hawkbill just hit a hydrophone! Just now! It's about six quadrants from you guys. That's a long way off! I suggest you launch immediately. Repeat; suggest you launch number 20 immediately!"

As Kent's transmission ended, Captain Smith of the Hawkbill ordered his boat down another hundred feet. It was time to give his crew and especially Grahams, his sonar man, a break from intense vigilance. He would staircase his sub down for a while at slow speed.

Trinola acknowledged Kent's message through his headset as his team broke through the final layer of ice. The blue water at the bottom of the ice hole gave way to a dark and ominous color. Working rapidly with practiced precision, they quickly prepared for another torpedo launch. The adrenaline rush of launching against a known target, even though relatively far away, put a smile of determination on their faces as they bent to the task at hand.

Far below and ninety degrees from a line between them and the Hawkbill, the dark hull of another submarine moved silently through the water, out of the range of the hydrophone field. It turned and headed for the pack ice ceiling. As it cleared a group of hanging stalactites, the blurry red star on its side came into focus. As the beams from its running lights intermittently reflected off ice formations, its Cyrillic number designation, K240, appeared. Soon only its tail panel with its two smoothly turning props was visible and then that, too, disappeared into the dark water as it moved in the same direction as the American sub.

On the packed ice surface, Trinola's team surveyed their recent breach.

"The ice is awfully thick here," Trinola said as he stared at the man-made opening. "Len, you better set the launcher for a deep release."

"Yeah, okay," Len replied. "Know how deep it is?"

Trinola guessed, "I'd say about eighteen feet. Jesus that's deeper than we've ever launched through."

Len adjusted the launcher and replied, "Well, that's two feet beyond our usual release depth. I am lengthening the start lanyard and steepening the entry angle. The torpedo should make it without tumbling the gyro." (I hope, he added to himself.)

Unlike the gyros on sophisticated fighter jets that maintained their reliability through multiple-G turns and upside down flight, the stabilizing gyros on a torpedo were simpler and required relatively level trajectory, at least at startup. A deep hole in the ice meant the gyros would be operating in an envelope beyond the optimum configurations they had been tested—and proven—within. Depending on the angle of the launch, there was a possibility the gyro servers could tumble, lose their orientation, and send the torpedo God-knows where.

Len adjusted the lanyard and the angle of the launcher, and the team lowered it down the hole. A light breeze rippled through the quadrupod, from which the launcher hung, causing the crew to grimace involuntarily, remembering the storm of the last few nights. But this time the wind was gentle, not strong enough to upset the balance of the torpedo. The ice was thick, and the hole was deep, but at least the weather wouldn't be a problem.

Trinola keyed the talk button on his walkie-talkie: "Kent, prepare for number 20 launch."

"Ready," Kent's voice rasped through the speaker, "anytime. Subs Archer and Ray positions noted and tracking. Hawk presumed hiding, the closest to you of the three, although last seen, quite a ways off."

Trinola gave the order, "OK. Launch in five, four, three, two, one. Fire!"

Len pulled the lanyard release and waited for what seemed longer than usual before the sound of torpedo activation and splashes of water came out of the launch hole. The team backed away. Underwater, the torpedo bounced off the lower rim of the ice hole, its props churning into ice, until it finally broke out in a downward erratic spiral at a steep attitude.

"Damn!" Trinola shouted. "It must have hit the bottom edge of the hole! Hope its sonar face isn't damaged."

Kent's voice again came through the loudspeaker: "Yeah, I think it took a few hits, but sounds like we have spiral search happening. I've got normal readings."

Trinola sighed in noticeable relief, "Okay, we'll stay here awhile. If there's no acquisition, we'll have to dig a shallower hole somewhere out here and try launching another one."

Trinola spoke into his microphone: "Kent, instead of having Rob and Jack snowmobile back for another torp, we might save some time by having you and Greg load one on the helo to bring out to us."

Kent countered, "Yeah, that might have worked, but the helicopter isn't back yet from Prudhoe Bay; something about picking up some VIP."

"OK," Trinola replied, "Just keep listening. Maybe number 20 will do its job, and we won't have to launch another. Keep me informed." Trinola put the walkie-talkie back down against his side, the strap holding it in place. VIP? He wondered to himself. NOW what?

"Roger. Out," confirmed Kent.

The silver-gray torpedo number 20, its sonar nose, scratched and slightly dented from its collision with the bottom of the ice hole, slowly spiraled down into deeper, darker waters. It seemed to be functioning adequately, though the collision with the ice had slightly scrambled its gyros, which were now spooling back to the proper speed. As the gyros corrected themselves, the torpedo's erratic pings briefly returned as echoes from an ominous moving silhouette.

It was the Soviet nuclear submarine K240. But the torpedo's slightly damaged echo receptors in its rubber nose failed to recognize the new target. It disregarded the target and continued its spiral search pattern, reporting nothing unusual to Kent listening on the surface.

*   *   *

The blue-lit helmsmen on the darkened bridge of the Soviet submarine slowly steered starboard in response to the voice of Capt. Leonid Glamouri. With over three decades in military service—and the pride and arrogance that naturally came with that experience—the fifty-three-year-old skipper's mastery was well known by both the Russian navy and United States naval intelligence.

"Starboard ten degrees, down attitude fifteen degrees," the captain's calm voice spoke quietly but firmly. Experience had taught him to be on his guard in these waters, and at his command the sub was in silent running mode. If there were mice around, he preferred to be the cat.

"Increase speed to twelve knots and level off in two minutes."

Despite having grown up in a politically connected family and all the privileges that came with it, Glamouri was a seasoned warrior respected by his crew. He was one of the first Russian commanders to guide a submarine through the treacherous undersea world of the Arctic and thus, was familiar with its ice floes above and mountainous ocean terrain below. His experience had even taught him the seasonal currents and thermo clines that are unique to the freezing ocean in that part of the world. A master of military strategy, Glamouri had skippered various classes of Russian submarines for the last twenty-one years.

In addition, Leonid Glamouri was also a celebrity in the rarified world of the Soviet military. Having first graduated top in his class of the prestigious Frunze Military Academy, he advanced quickly through a pilot program where he discovered his career's passion for submarines. Some say he was driven to excel to distance himself from the influence of a strong mother who had arranged a marriage for her reluctant son. Others said he was short tempered and arrogant because of it. In any event, most of his life was spent at sea and very rarely at the side of his socialite wife. They had no children. In Glamouri's mind his crew was his family, to be disciplined, molded, and readied for the challenges they would inevitably face. "That is what this Cold War will come down to," he had once told his crew. "Better get ready for battle."

Slightly taller than most of his direct subordinates, Glamouri dressed impeccably and sported a well trimmed white beard which contrasted dramatically against his black woolen sweater, with its captain's insignia—a gold hammer and sickle over a silver anchor—pinned near the neck. It was not only Glamouri's prestigious military biography that gained him loyal respect, but the confident way he moved his elegantly postured body as he commanded the ship. Glamouri's confident authority bred allegiance and discipline in his crew. But at this particular moment, the captain, despite all his experience and confidence, needed to hit the head.

"Take over Mishky," the Soviet captain said, turning to his second-in-command. "I'll be back in ten minutes. But repeat the same maneuver in precisely seven."

Snapping to attention, young Lieut. Mishky took the command position on the bridge. "Yes sir, Captain!" Mishky, thirty-five years old with a boyish face, had been in Glamouri's command for only two years but well understood his position, including its past. As he took command of the bridge he remembered the man he replaced, who was sanctioned and removed from duty for failing Glamouri for some unknown offense.

Mishky was an obedient and effective second-in-command, as much for self-preservation as for duty. And Mishky had gained at least some respect and leniency from his captain, having graduated from the same Frunze Military Academy. Gramouri had specifically asked for him after he read Mishky's academy service report, a fact that Mishky never forgot. He hoped he would never give his captain reason to regret that decision.

Five minutes, and counting, he said to himself as he looked at his watch.

*   *   *

The damaged American torpedo, still pinging in the general direction of the Soviet sub, turned toward it randomly, receiving a few positive echoes. It pinged several more times, then came alive with a straight heading toward the sub. Its seeker head damage was apparently slight, and such a large target had finally burned through to the undamaged receptors. The torpedo increased its speed to chase mode. But after several more pings, the damaged circuits fought back, confusing the computer, and the seeker head abruptly went silent. The torpedo slowed and began another circular search, its ping rate intermittent, and its engine vibrating with erratic prop rotations.

Seven minutes had passed. Mishky crisply ordered the submarine into another starboard turn with down fifteen-degree angle, increasing speed, duplicating the captain's last maneuver.

The torpedo kept circling slowly, its computer attempting to make sense of the conflicting inputs from both the damaged seeker head and undamaged receptors. Another group of echoes returned off the Russian sub. Once again the torpedo locked on, increased speed, and performed its helix transition out of its circle search. The torpedo was in pursuit.

*   *   *

Onboard the green-lit helm of the USS Hawkbill, sonar man Grahams yelled, "Skipper, we've got another active torpedo, right out of nowhere. Jesus! Wait! ...checking now.

"NO! This time I know for sure it didn't come from either the Archerfish or Ray!"

Staring intently into his scope and noting the incoming, ever changing information as it appeared in front of him, Grahams continued his data narration, "Just starting to hear more pings and maybe speed change. Not sure."

Capt. Smith turned toward Grahams' visibly tense posture, "What's the heading?"

Grahams replied, "Can't be sure of that yet, Captain, but I know it could not have been launched from the Ray or Archerfish. They are far behind us, and this thing is somewhere off our starboard bow."

Capt. Smith turned back to his helmsman, "Clancy, slow to one-quarter."

"One-quarter, Sir," Clancy replied, easing back on the throttle controls.

"Captain, sounds like those pings are being reflected off the...

SHIT!...there's another sub out there!" Turning away from his console, his confusion showing, Grahams looked directly at the captain. "Can there be another sub, Sir?"

Capt. Smith shook his head and gave orders to Clancy, "Steady as she goes. If that torpedo's coming across our bow, let's keep it there. Keep a small profile."

Grahams spoke again, excited, "Got it skipper. Definitely another sub. Increasing speed. It's being chased by that torpedo! Sounds like sub just started turning toward us. Damn! That's just what it's doing!"

"Slow to one-eighth, Clancy." The captain urged." Grahams, can you get a LOWFAR [Low frequency acoustic record] profile on that sub and make out who it is?"

"I'll try, Captain!"

                    *   *   *

The Russian submarine turned to port, increasing speed from right to left across the Hawkbill's bow; the pinging torpedo following in the distance. The sounds of the torpedo pinging against the Russian submarine intensified on the bridge as the tempo of the race increased. The torpedo was operating normally now, its computer settling on the correct inputs and ignoring the data from the damaged seeker head. Seemingly invigorated by the chase, the parts of the machine worked in harmony, props turning rapidly, and control fins adjusting, guiding the torpedo toward its kill.

                    *   *   *

In the blue-lit helm of the Russian sub, Capt. Glamouri re-entered the bridge area, his personal bathroom duties completed. One glance at his lieutenant and he instantly recognized a crisis.

"Mishky, what the hell is going on?"

The crew stiffened as Glamouri appeared, a normal reaction for a crew diligent to its captain's rigorous demands, but more so this time because of the audibly increasing torpedo pings.

Lieut. Mishky replied quickly, "Being followed by a torpedo, Sir. I turned full port and am currently speeding up to full!"

Capt. Glamouri, nodding his assent, said, "Good. Three degrees more left rudder. Let's head for the Alpha Cordillera ice forms and lose that damn thing! Quick men! Every moment counts."

*　　　*　　　*

The Soviet sub turned toward its new bearing. The duel propellers churned, overcoming its massive double-hull resistance. The Delta III-class submarine had twice the nuclear power of the American subs in order to compensate for its extra displacement. It accelerated slightly slower, but once up to full speed the K240 almost matched the Hawkbill, less by just one knot. But one knot could make all the difference when running for the cover of submerged blocks of ice.

Torpedo number 20 was locked on Glamouri's submarine, adjusting its plane and vertical fins in response to the sub's every move. The props of the K240 spun up like skidding tires, trying to propel the submarine forward. The props cavitated, producing bubbles at the trailing edges of their blades, until the submarine accelerated to its maximum speed. The noise of cavitation was temporarily noticeable above the higher pitch whine of the sub's duel steam turbines. The distinctive noise propagated through otherwise quiet waters: rapid popcorn-popping sounds as the water vapor bubbles formed and then collapsed under ocean pressures.

*　　　*　　　*

On board the Hawkbill, Grahams called out, "Got it Captain! From my LOWFAR profile manual it's got to be the USSR-K240. Its last known skipper, a Leonid Glamouri."

"Can it still be Glamouri?" the captain shook his head in disbelief. "He's one of the first Russian guys to drive a missile-loaded sub through the surface of the Arctic ice pack. Think it was back in 1981. If it's really Glamouri, then we have one very aggressive and paranoid skipper on our hands!"

"Yeah," Lieut. Maple quickly added. "Isn't he the Ruskie skipper who first accused our Glomar Explorer of trying to salvage their sunken K129 sub in '74?"

"Same guy. Their sub sank in 1968 due to a missile malfunction," said Capt. Smith. "And the Glomar Explorer found her in '74 off Hawaii at sixteen thousand feet while supposedly mining for manganese nodules—some kind of CIA cover story. Glamouri's suspicions were able to put it all together and alert some high ranking Russian admiral who hardly gave him any credit!"

Lieut. Maple recalled, "Right! I remember that 'looking-for-nodules' cover story the CIA used for …wasn't it… 'Project Jennifer' to recover Soviet code books and nuclear missiles—which I heard they did. I bet that really pissed off Glamouri, if he ever found out."

"That might be the case," Grahams added, "Cause it seems like he's coming right toward us! Going to cross our port bow in less than seven minutes at his current speed."

"Damn," Captain Smith replied, moving to his command table. "If that's really Glamouri, no telling what he'll do when he sees us, or one of our other submarines!

"Actually, I know EXACTLY what he'll do: He'll think WE shot that torpedo at him, and he'll fire back at us, or at our guys. And one thing will be for sure: he'll be firing lethal torpedoes!"

"Clancy, all stop," the captain ordered, a worried look creasing his face. "Up periscope one-quarter. L-LITE on. I know I won't be able to see much, but I have to be sure."

The periscope emerged just enough to clear the sail as Smith got on his knees to look through it. Operating the device with both hands, and peering into the face scope, Smith kept talking. "Grahams, if that's Glamouri, he knows the formations of Alpha-Cordillera better than any man alive. And he will come our way to use them to break trail and hide! So give me an indication. I need something to confirm it!"

"Aye-aye, Sir," an anxious Grahams replied.

"And you, Clancy, get ready for full speed and up incline to intercept that torpedo."

"Yes Sir."

Through his headset, Grahams, could clearly hear torpedo pings and changes of frequency, and he yelled loud enough for everyone to hear, "Torpedo pursuit switch, Captain! And Sov sub definitely turning our way."

Peering through the periscope, Captain Smith saw a dim and blurry profile of the Soviet submarine, making a turn, heading across his bow toward his port side. Although designed for above-surface night vision, the Kollmorgen Type-18 periscope was fitted with a Low-Light Image Intensified Television (L-LITE) system that offered crude underwater imagery. Not very clear, but clear enough.

Capt. Smith rose up off his knees. "Damn it! Definitely Soviet. Down scope."

Grahams yelled out, "Confirmation. Captain, he's coming our way!"

"Christ!" Smith replied, angrily, "I knew it! Clancy, full speed ahead, incline twenty degrees."

"And battle stations!"

The captain bit down hard on his lip, trying to make his brain think faster. It did. "Let's intercept that torpedo. We've got to prevent an international crisis, boys!"

Speaking rapidly, the captain gave his orders, "Let's try to have the torpedo acquire us before it switches to attack frequency. We've got to get between the torp and that Soviet sub, and then Glamouri, or whoever it is, will understand what we're doing and not retaliate."

*   *   *

The Soviet sub and the torpedo were both racing toward the Hawkbill. The Hawkbill was accelerating to top speed to intercept the torpedo and shield the enemy sub. It would be a tricky maneuver, and Captain Smith would need all his experience and a little luck for Hawkbill to lead the torpedo away from the Soviets.

*   *   *

On the surface, an otherwise lovely day on the Arctic ice, Trinola and his launch team waited at the launch hole. Curious how the torpedo was functioning, Trinola called the communications hut, "Kent, what's happening with 20? Do we need to launch another?"

Kent replied, his words tripping over each other in his excitement, "No Sir! Torpedo 20 has acquired a sub. But you won't believe this. It's not one of ours!"

"What?" asked Trinola, his body tensing. "Whose is it? Canadian or British? Can they be informed of our tests?"

Kent called back, "Well, Spiry here first thought it was British. But as far as Greg and I can tell from our hydrophone traces and scant LOWFAR manual comparisons it's a pretty large Soviet sub, delta missile class."

"Crap!" Trinola yelled, "Well now THAT'S just perfect! I guess number 20 wasn't damaged that much during launch. It acquired. If that's really a Russian sub, we should start praying that for once our torp doesn't switch to attack mode. The sooner it turns away the less likely we'll be held responsible for a major international incident. Assuming it turns away at all. Damn. I don't believe this!"

Overhearing Trinola's alarm, Len hurried over and asked, "What's going on?"

"Well, you better start praying that number 20 somehow shuts down, because it's headed for a Soviet sub," Trinola replied, the disgust clear in his voice. "It's out of our hands now!"

It's out of our hands now. The words resonated in Trinola's head, changing his composure as if he was somehow relieved of a burden he'd been carrying since the project began. He took a deep breath and sighed with unexpected relief. His mind raced to the future. Whatever was going to happen next will affect the entire project, probably my career, and maybe even curtail further torpedo programs at NOSC, San Diego. But it's out of my hands now, he repeated to himself. The quiet dread he had been feeling much of the past few months finally had no hold on him.

"There's nothing more we can do here, Kent," Trinola said into his walkie-talkie. "We'll put all the equipment in the tool shed and head back to camp. The hilo can pick it up when it's back from escorting that VIP."

"Roger that," Kent replied, wondering what was behind his boss's sudden perfunctory tone. "See you back at camp."

*　　　*　　　*

The blue lights of the helm in the Russian sub reflected off the troubled face of Capt. Glamouri as he leaned over a map of the area. His already tense crewmen jumped when he yelled, "Get us into those Alpha ice forms Mishky!"

Mishky started shouting out orders for bearing, depth and speed as Capt. Glamouri fired questions into the ear of his sonar man, "What's the range of that torpedo? What's its speed? When will it intercept us?"

"Not sure Captain. Maybe about two thousand meters. But it's closing fast, Sir. Contact in another three and a half minutes."

The sonar man leaned toward his scope, not quite believing what he was seeing. "Something else, Captain. Seems…seems to be a sub heading for us, thirty degrees off our portside."

"Ours?" Capt. Glamouri quickly asked.

"No, sir. Sounds like American." Then, after a pause, "Yes, definitely, American."

Capt. Glamouri ran back to the helm. "Try and get a profile if you can!" Turning to Mishky, the captain shouted, "We've got an American sub heading for us!"

Mishky asked the obvious: "Why would the sub be heading back in the direction it launched the torpedo?"

"I don't know," Glamouri replied, running his hands through his hair. When he looked up, a new expression had come over his face. "Wait...maybe it didn't launch the torpedo! Maybe another sub did."

"You mean we're surrounded?" asked Mishky, fear welling up from his gut and causing his voice to break its usually smooth cadence.

"Forget the American submarine," Glamouri scolded, but in a somehow reassuring voice. "Our first priority is to lose that torpedo and whatever else they think of throwing at us! We'll be in the thick of Alpha formations soon, safe from whoever and whatever.

"Up periscope, on LITC [the Russian version of Light Intensified Television Camera]! One-quarter speed."

*   *   *

The Soviet sub, with its periscope emerging, headed for the protection of dense ice formations, the American torpedo in determined pursuit. With the sound of its engines and propeller intensifying, the Hawkbill closed the distance to intercept the torpedo as erratic formations of ice came into partial view.

The huge ice formations, under a momentary cracked ice pack, glowed with penetrating streams of daylight breaking through, illuminating the USSR-K240, the trailing torpedo, and the USS Hawkbill-666. The speed of each was accelerating, the distance between them closing.

*   *   *

Onboard the Hawkbill, Capt. Smith asked, "Grahams, you have those interception coordinates yet?"

"Got 'em Captain. Forty-three degrees by six. Wait! Russian sub just turned starboard toward Alpha Dome crevice. Torpedo following! New intercept for torpedo—thirty-eight degrees by 5.2..."

*   *   *

The Soviet sub turned toward four giant ice formations, one at each corner of a large dome that hollowed out the ceiling of the ice pack. The ice forms like sentries guarded the dome. Capt Glamouri intended to enter between two of them and snuggle up into the dome, an ideal place to hide from the torpedo.

The Hawkbill adjusted its bearing to intercept the torpedo, its propeller screaming at maximum attack speed.

Chapter 11

Suspicion to Paranoia

Onboard the Russian Sub, Capt. Glamouri peered through his periscope and winced with an audible sigh. What he saw was an American submarine turning from an attack pursuit of his own sub toward another trajectory, one that could only leave a single conclusion. "I can't believe it, that American sub is heading right for the torpedo! Have we got an audio profile yet?"

"Yes, Captain," his sonar man replied, "It's the USS Hawkbill. And according to my calculations it...it appears to be heading to intercept the torpedo!"

Lieut. Mishky stared at the sonar man, then back to his captain, a confused look on his face. "It's putting itself at risk, Captain? That is strange. Doesn't he know we're about to break trail in these ice forms?

Mishky continued speaking, thinking as he walked toward the captain and the sonar man: "Why would he be...? Unless he deliberately wants to protect us, Captain. That must be it, Sir. He is sacrificing himself, or maybe going to disarm the torpedo to somehow prevent what might become a crisis!"

Capt. Glamouri shook his head, disbelieving what he was seeing and now hearing. "If that is so, then why did he fire a torpedo at us in the first place."

"With due respect, my Captain," Mishky replied, gathering

courage to continue, "With all due respect, Sir, remember you said that he probably wasn't the one who launched it. Maybe another U.S. sub launched it by mistake."

"That would be two, too many 'ifs,' Lieutenant," the captain growled back. "Maybe he wasn't the one who launched it, but he might be positioning himself to launch his own torpedo at us right now. Maybe what we're seeing is exactly what they intended...our destruction!"

The captain moved quickly back to his command table. "I can't afford to jeopardize my ship and crew for the wrong ifs, especially by trying to outguess this Hawkbill captain. I can't afford to guess wrong!"

Looking around the control room at his crew, he said, slowly, "Always think the worst; that is my policy."

More loudly this time, the captain ordered, "After we break torpedo trail, we're going to do the only thing that makes sense. Glamouri hesitated, while those listening could only imagine what that might be.

"We can't let these Americans overcome us up here. I haven't acquired my position after all these years by just hiding! I—WE—own these ice fields!"

The helmsman slowed the Soviet sub to negotiate between two of the giant ice formations that edged one end of the ice dome. Following his captain's orders, the helmsman cut the engines, and the sub coasted in silence, out of acoustic sight. "Slower still, helmsman," Capt. Glamouri urged. "We don't want to overshoot our cover by having to reverse engines, or worse yet, break through the top of the ice dome!"

Every sailor in the control room knew that breaking the surface would create enormous acoustical signals for any American sub listening nearby, and more importantly, defeat their purpose of breaking trail and hiding from the pursuing torpedo. The noise of metal on ice would be as noticeable to the torpedo's sensitive receptors as it would be to the ears of an American sonar man.

Despite its defensive maneuvers, the Soviet sub had not broken contact with American torpedo No. 20, which continued to head directly toward K240. The torpedo's onboard computer ignored the frequency changes of returning pings bouncing off the ice that now partially hid the sub. The torpedo was working perfectly, too close to be fooled. It was locked on, and determined to make a kill.

Glamouri's sonar man, his voice shaking, whispered the torpedo's coordinates in Russian equivalents,
"280 yards...260 .... 230...."

*　　　*　　　*

As the torpedo closed in on the Russian sub, the Hawkbill closed in on the torpedo, coming up at a thirty degree incline. Either by its initial damage or by the heat of pursuit, the torpedo was oblivious to the presence of the Hawkbill. All it could see was the Russian submarine.

*　　　*　　　*

On board the Hawkbill, Capt. Smith pictured the external scene in his mind. Imagining angles and closing distances as only a well experienced sub commander could, he whispered to count of audible pings, took a deep breath, and yelled out, "Level off Clancy!

"Brace yourselves, men, just in case that dummy torpedo doesn't turn away in time!"

*　　　*　　　*

The torpedo did not turn away in time. It had reached the 200 yard distance from the Soviet sub and had begun its decelerating turn away. Its seeker head suddenly caught the returning pings of a new target, huge and dead ahead. The Hawkbill was already inside the torp's 200 yard turn away limit. The torp's computer could not negotiate the new data and respond before the American sub ran right in front of it. The torpedo sideswiped the sub with a loud grinding noise. The sub lurched, temporarily off balance, its crewmen struggling to steady themselves. Then there was silence.

The Hawkbill continued its full-speed and direction. Captain Smith now wanted to put some distance between his ship and the Soviet sub, which was less than two hundred yards away. The torpedo's trajectory arched downward, its previously damaged gyros attempting to right themselves, but not able to spool up fast enough to gain operative speed. The torpedo spiraled deeper into the darkness, erratic as if drunk. At its present rate of descent, it would soon be crushed by the depth pressures of the Arctic. So deep it would not be heard by listening ears—a cold silent death.

*   *   *

"Damage report!" The Hawkbill captain yelled. One by one, each station radioed the all-clear.

Lieut. Maple reported, "All seems secure, Captain! Probably the worst thing is some deep scratches on the hull, but nothing to be concerned about. Hull secure. She hit us far from the sail or any vulnerable hatches."

The captain relaxed, then stiffened, a broad smile breaking over his face. "We did it!" the somewhat surprised captain exclaimed, catching his crewmen with unexpected audible—and uncharacteristic—joy. "Maybe that'll satisfy those Russians."

A visibly relieved Captain Smith smiled toward his helmsman. "Now, slow to one-half and start port circle till we hear from those Russians."

*   *   *

The Russian sub pulled out of its hiding place between the hanging ice, gained speed and dove deep. The crew heard the torpedo hit the Hawkbill, and Glamouri reviewed his strategy. He commanded full speed and a steep dive angle out of the dome. Better to flee the Hawkbill now, Glamouri thought to himself, while it's still pondering its next move.

K240 took on depth at its steepest dive angle and moved farther away from the dome. The Soviet captain watched the depth gauge spool down, noting the fathoms as the sub pressed toward its operating depth. The crew at the com braced themselves, anticipating impulsive directives, knowing Glamouri's emotions were getting the best of him. Tension drew beads of sweat upon their brows until their worst expectations were fulfilled.

*   *   *

Glamouri slammed his fist onto his table and yelled out to his helmsman. "Reverse dive. Take us up, back to the dome. Full speed! Maximum angle!

"My v bitvakh reshayem...[In battles we shall decide...]" Glamouri's words trailed off to a whisper.

The helmsman turned to see his captain's face, needing to confirm his latest orders. He didn't have to wait.

"Damn it, I said full speed, take us up!" the captain screamed.

All eyes turned toward Lieutenant Mishky, knowing if anyone had enough guts to question the captain's command, it would be him. But Glamouri's stern resolve stared down any possible argument Mishky might voice.

The sub headed back to the dome, as the captain called for up periscope. He identified the beams of light breaking through weak points in the surface ice and guided his helmsman toward them. The sub headed for the surface, increasing speed.

"Crew, brace for breach!" the lieutenant ordered through the com. He did not ask for permission from his captain, whose angry face was peering through the scope.

"Down scope!" Glamouri yelled out. Grabbing hold of the scope's stanchions, he turned again to Mishky, breaking a soft smile of satisfaction.

*   *   *

The sub broached the ice pack with a crashing sound—heard and felt—by the entire crew, its sail clearing the watery ice. Like the whale of the deep it most resembled, the sub settled quickly back into the surface of the broiling water. It slowed, its sail and Russian insignias glowing in blue reflections of the sun off the nearby ice.

*   *   *

"Jesus!" The Hawkbill's sonar man shouted, ripping off his headsets against the amplified sounds of the Soviet sub's breach. "He came up, and fast, captain!"

"New course, straight on to that Russian sub!" Captain Smith shouted, and the Hawkbill turned in pursuit. "Take us up, max speed, helmsman!" He added, gripping his table tightly as the sub surged in a high angle. Pencils rolled onto the floor and coffee cups spilled as crewmen grabbed at them before reconsidering and holding onto their chairs instead.

In a display of a submarine's ability to power through any hindrance, the Hawkbill broached through the ice pack, its nose breaking through first, then its sail. The sub dramatically crashed down into the icy water, quietly settling into a level attitude. Capt. Smith quickly ascended the spiral stairs to the sail, opened the hatch, and scanned west, looking for the Soviet sub. His binoculars confirmed his astonishment. The two subs were so close that each captain could see his rival peering back through binoculars at the other. Capt. Smith quickly recognized the white beard of the notorious Captain Glamouri. He could hardly believe his eyes.

"Of all the three-hundred Soviet subs we had to get involved with," the captain said to his lieutenant, now joining him and pulling out his own binoculars, "This guy is the most arrogant maverick of them all! No telling what he'll do now.

"Lieut. Maple, Call to battle stations!"

*   *   *

Glamouri stood atop his sub and peered through his binoculars. He scanned past the Hawkbill—and its captain—and looked to the east of the American sub. To his amazement, he saw a large ice camp in the distance. Glamouri grumbled to himself then turned to his second officer. "Send a message to Soviet Command, and I don't care if the Americans hear it. Tell them our situation and inform them of a new target for our forces. A military land installation, just east of that sub."

"But Sir," Lieutenant Mishky timidly replied, "Shouldn't we encode our transmissions?"

"Do what I tell you, sailor! Send the following:

USSR-K240 torpedoed by USS Hawkbill. Two missiles set and readied upon New York and Washington targets. Awaiting permission to launch missiles.

"Send it now! Unencrypted!"

*   *   *

The communications officer on The Hawkbill sat bolt upright, having never heard a live Russian transmission before. He noted the frequency that his scanners had picked up, double checking again before he spoke, just as Captain Smith and Lieutenant Maple descended onto the bridge.

"Captain, Sir! Receiving live Russian transmission. And I think it's from that sub!"

"Translation?" the captain yelled back.

"Working on it, Sir." The com officer wrote furiously, translating the words he knew while his language software slowly put together the sentences in English. Finished, he stood and practically ran the few steps to the captain's table.

Captain Smith read the note, visibly startled at the words on the paper.

"Hell, things have gotten out of hand, people!" The captain reported loudly, handing the paper to his lieutenant. "Glamouri's next move is anybody's guess! Doesn't he know I just saved his ass?"

God help us, he added, under his breath.

Lieut. Maple offered, "Just like a blind bugger not to accept an act of redemption for what it is!"

On the bridge of the Soviet submarine, Glamouri impatiently waited for a reply from headquarters. He had already ordered two missile doors opened, revealing the gleaming white nose cones of intercontinental missiles. To anyone looking, he wanted to show he meant business.

A U.S. helicopter was the first to notice. Coming from the ice camp to investigate, it quickly turned back when the pilot recognized the Soviet insignia on the sail of the submarine. The pilot increased his speed as his co-pilot pointed at the two open missile doors. The helicopter crew wanted no part of what was about to happen.

*   *   *

Lieutenant Mishky stepped away from the communications desk, a printout in his hand. "Sir, this just came in from Soviet intelligence."

"Soviet intelligence?" The captain asked. "What do I care what Soviet intelligence said! We work for Soviet command! What did command say?!"

"Sir, I think this IS actually from command."

"Read it, Lieutenant. Out loud."

The lieutenant looked around at his subordinates. Another breach in protocol, he thought to himself. What would the political officer think about that when he makes his report. He cleared his throat, and read:

> Informant from U.S. camp just confirmed: U.S. torpedo games in the Arctic have been going on for several weeks. They are only war games with dummy torpedoes. TAKE NO OFFENSIVE ACTION. DO NOT LAUNCH MISSILES. Vacate area immediately, before more test torpedoes acquire and prove vulnerability of Soviet submarines. *Plivy s muzjestvom ...V silje spokojnoje!* [Sail with courage...Calm in strength!]

*　　　*　　　*

"What is this, a party line?" The com officer on the Hawkbill said out loud. "Captain, another un-encrypted message. This time it's going TO that Russky sub."

Captain Smith read the message and started to speak, but turned his head up toward the open hatch on the sail. The sound of an approaching helicopter came through, its rotors sounding close. Captain Smith climbed up the ladder and stood on the sail, noting the nonmilitary ICE-X markings on the approaching chopper. Joining him again, his lieutenant said loudly, against the sound of the rotors, "It's one of ours Sir. It's probably from that base camp a couple miles east." In that moment the lieutenant suddenly understood. "Captain, I think they are the ones who have been launching torpedoes."

"Get me a radio," the captain ordered, and the lieutenant reached and turned the handle of the nearby com box, extracting a telephone receiver. He dialed the device to a pre-set frequency, and handed it to his captain.

"Helicopter, this is the USS Hawkbill. What say you?" the captain spoke into the radio.

"Hawkbill, we're from the American base camp nearby. The war games are over. Stand down and prepare for executive boarding." As the transmission started to break up, Captain Smith heard, "We just have to complete one... fly ove...Russ.... Sure. Okay with you...."

"Affirmative," the captain replied, spontaneously assuming what he heard from the broken transmission and deciding to stir the pot. 'In for a penny, in for a pound,' he thought. "Yeah, a low fly-by over that submarine would be great. Just give them a friendly wave, if you don't mind."

"Roger that," the pilot retorted, turning his chopper back toward the Soviet ship. Captain Smith picked up his binoculars and peered back at the sub, noting that its missile doors had been closed and that the sub was beginning to move off.

Steaming with anger, the Russian captain looked at the American helicopter approaching his sail.

Glamouri glowered at the Americans on board as the chopper hovered within yards of his ship. His eyes locked intensely on those of the passengers, but one in particular—the only one in a bright green parka. The two stared at each other for a moment.

Glamouri's emotions overcame him. In frustration and broken pride, he gestured with a clenched fist, hammering his arm toward the helicopter, "Damn you Americans!"

"My k slave Otchiznu svoyu povedyom! [We shall lead to the glory of the Motherland!]"

His gesture mimicked the hammer and sickle, the Russian insignia that gleamed prominently on the side of his ship's sail. Glamouri was fuming as he descended down through the sail. The hatch closed over his head with a loud noise covering any further words he had to say.

With a rumble of engines, the K240 broke away from the grip of the icy surface and submerged into dark waters.

The U.S. helicopter turned back toward the Hawkbill and circled a few times, preparing to land some fifty yards away from the cracked ice around the submarine. As the helicopter's rotors spun down, its occupants stepped out and walked toward the Hawkbill. Behind them two snowmobiles from camp headed in their direction.

Closing the distance to the sub one of the men yelled, "Mission complete. War games over, captain. Permission for executive boarding?" Captain Smith shouted in return, "Permission granted."

*   *   *

Honors

Minutes later, the helicopter's entourage—including Alex Trinola, Capt. Clifford Dredge, and the man in the green parka,—climbed up and into the Hawkbill, which was floating in makeshift mooring against the broken ice.

The scene inside the bridge of the Hawkbill became a mix of strict military discipline and absolute awe. Every officer on the bridge was standing at rigid attention, except for the sonar man, who held in his arms a thick, green parka. He had taken the coat on orders from his captain, who snapped to attention when the man who wore the parka climbed down the ladder and pulled back the hood of his coat.

Secretary of the Navy, John F. Lehman Jr., smiled as he looked around at the men, all staring straight ahead, arms rigidly at their sides, in deference to their civilian commander. Only Capt. Smith had allowed himself a brief moment of noticeable perplexity at the unexpected arrival of his guest before calling himself to order. Smith then stepped back to the center of the room, saluting unnecessarily once again.

"At ease, sailors. I've come to throw a little praise around," Secretary Lehman stated, a little too loudly for the close quarters, but consistent with his well-known forcefulness. "You all have done good work. Great work, in fact. As of now, consider yourselves—and this fine ship of yours—up for the Meritorious Unit Commendation. It comes with a couple weeks of R&R, though hopefully at a more hospitable venue than what I just came in from."

"And beyond the official commendation, it must be said to you men, and you specifically, Captain Smith, that your acts of bravery and sacrifice helped mitigate an international incident."

The captain and his crew listened intently, not sure what to do with the mixed emotions that were welling up as the Secretary began to describe the reasons for their recent forays into gut-wrenching fear.

"Unbeknownst to you, for the past few weeks the U.S. Navy has been involved in war games with an experimental weapon, a torpedo, to be precise, that you may have noticed following your ship a couple times." The Secretary smiled, attempting to make light of the situation, not really noticing that he was the only one enjoying the levity.

The captain winced at the Secretary's light-hearted comment, silently hoping his full report would clue the man in to the trauma Mr. Lehman's "games" had on his crew.

"You should know, and be proud," the Secretary continued, "that all of the torpedoes in our test acquired and pursued their targets until the 200-yard turn away as programmed. That's right, a shortened turn away distance to ensure credibility. They performed exactly as they had been designed. Without exception."

Secretary Lehman summarized, "None of the submarines, including that Soviet sub, could evade detection or successfully break trail."

As he was speaking, the rest of Trinola's team climbed down into the bridge of the Hawkbill, crowding the small room to capacity. Apparently, the Secretary had wanted to include Alex's team in his remarks and not speak to the entire base camp.

As Alex's men interspersed themselves among the sailors, still at attention, Secretary Lehman turned toward Trinola. "Congratulations to you, Mr. Trinola and your torpedo team; for you have proven the vulnerability of the U.S. submarine fleet. And by a lucky coincidence, have shown that Russians subs are also vulnerable. Job well done."

Captain Smith eyed Trinola and thought to himself, 'So this is the guy responsible for all our speculations and worry. Not at all the sinister type of fellow I expected, but still an admirable foe nonetheless.' Smith almost said out loud, 'I can't wait to find out how you launched those torps at us through the ice.'

Lehman turned back to the captain, abruptly changing his demeanor to one of noticeable seriousness. "Capt. Smith, you and the skippers of the submarines Ray and Archerfish, were intentionally not given the turn-away distance of the torpedoes in order to guarantee your best efforts at evasive tactics. That was my decision to break precedent. I know that couldn't possibly sit well with you and your men, but it had to be done. Secrecy was of utmost importance, as was your true reaction to a real torpedo attack. We had to test these torpedoes against sub crews whose lives depended on their defensive actions. Real time reactions against real threats. There was no other way.

"And Mr. Trinola, what you may have perceived to be a dubious and dangerous decision not to disclose everything to the submariners, well, actually turned out in your favor. For it did indeed prove the capabilities of your torpedoes beyond any doubt.

"You probably didn't know the global significance of your mission, but your fortitude in its completion was admirable. I've been personally following the results of the tests, and informing the President accordingly."

Trinola stepped forward, still not clear about all his feelings toward the Secretary, but trying to let his explanations assure him and calm his anger. "You're right, Mr. Secretary, about my fear of what could've gone wrong, especially when it came to that Russian sub. In fact, when I saw its missile hatches open, I thought that was the end of everything."

Capt. Smith added, "I did too! I am still trying to figure out why that arrogant Glamouri backed down, even with orders direct from Soviet command. I was afraid he might fire those missiles anyway."

Lehman smiled thinly, gathering his thoughts before speaking. These men had been pushed to the breaking point, and he didn't want to push them further. "Well, gentlemen, I have a confession to make, but...."

The Secretary stopped short, looked around at those who might be hearing his next words, smiled, and settled his eyes upon Captain Smith. "Captain, would you please excuse your crew except your lieutenant here?" At Captain Smith's nod, the bridge crew filed out and closed the bulkhead door; Secretary Lehman thanked them as they exited.

Lehman turned and smiled again at Captain Smith, looking at the others before he continued. "To provide a little insurance against Soviet involvement, we planted a Soviet spy, an informant at ice camp, named Ross Spiry. Through him, they knew these were just tests. And we were strongly relying on their diligence to keep things in perspective. I guess that paid off, even though that three-day storm compromised communications."

Trinola and his team stirred visibly, each man remembering a different experience or encounter with Spiry, each realizing how suddenly it all made sense. But what a chance to take! Thought Trinola. Our new technology could have been compromised! Above my pay grade, I guess.

Lehman continued, "Oh. And Mr. Trinola, I told Capt. Dredge here, about Spiry the day you guys left my office last year. I told him Spiry had a good track record of feeding info we wanted known."

Lehman glanced at Dredge and nodded, Trinola and his team noticing the gesture. Trinola wondered how much more of this he could take. What was really being tested, he asked himself, my torpedoes or my men?

The Secretary looked back at Trinola with a smile, "I needed somebody to really keep me informed, and make sure Spiry would be protected to do his informant job. I found out about the heater sabotage and fire, both incidents initiated by Spiry. I'm sorry, but Capt. Dredge was sworn to secrecy, since we had to protect Spiry from being detected. Dredge was on your side all along!"

Trinola could no longer keep silent, "And where is Spiry now?"

Lehman nodded. "To protect our investment, we're already sending him back to Washington with the first wave of departing personnel from camp, probably as we speak. He's already been given some false info for our next project. A Soviet spy like him is invaluable in these precarious times.

"You'd be surprised how much we've learned by using spies in military operation such as these. Hopefully, with this test proving another level of technical superiority over the Soviet fleet, their need will diminish. We've beaten them again, and at some point we hope they'll stop trying.

"But more importantly, your torpedo team has shown once again how reliable and critical our scientists and engineers are to the security of our nation. Only time will tell the full strategic significance of these tests at the top of the world— how they will influence the course of history. You all did your jobs, and you have my thanks. And your country's gratitude."

*   *   *

Torpedo Triumph

Deep within the dark icy waters, torpedo number 20's electrical circuitry awoke from its stupor. Its gyros finally had spooled to a stable rotation, and the onboard computer had ordered a stop to the torpedo's descent. The rear fins guided the torp back toward the surface. It soon began its circular search pattern, pinging toward the fleeing Soviet submarine. Pulling level at its predetermined depth, the torpedo straightened out and increased its speed. It was again in pursuit of USSR-K240, closing range as Secretary of the Navy Lehman finished congratulating those who participated in the torpedo tests.

Sometime later, at precisely 200 yards distance, the torpedo might break track and circle back to its retrieval point. That wasn't for sure, but one thing was: one more scare for the crew of the Soviet sub, and the convincing of an angry Russian commander that someone in Soviet command would hear no end to his rage.

*   *   *

"The military and civilian leaders of the Department of Defense had thought the U.S. submarine fleet was four years behind the strength of the Soviets," Secretary Lehman was winding up his remarks to the men gathered in the Hawkbill. "But what we've learned today says otherwise. Instead, these tests indicate we do not need more subs to patrol Arctic waters against hiding Russian subs. We now know that just a few subs and capable torpedoes can search and find them.

"But gentlemen, the greater significance of these tests is that President Reagan's buildup of the Navy—maybe the entire military— can be reversed, since our worst threat is now mitigated. You guys have proven that 'Peace through Strength' has already been achieved."

*   *   *

Six months after the Arctic tests, a summit meeting between Reagan and Gorbachev at Reykjavik, Iceland, resolved to reduce the number of intermediate-range nuclear missiles on both sides. The end of the Cold War had begun.

Years later, Trinola would note the Arctic torpedo tests of ICE-X '86 actually involved 23 torpedoes, all of which successfully acquired their submarine targets. The tests of 1986 helped prove the efficacy of President Ronald Reagan's policy of "Peace through Strength" and justified his thirty-five percent increase in defense spending. President Reagan's policy of strength produced the undersea tactical capabilities America needed to ensure peace at the top of the world.

Epilogue

The Torpedo Team Today:

Even after twenty-five years, most of the men in Trinola's team meet annually for lunch in San Diego, California. Trinola, Len, and Rob are retired, but everyone involved recalls the importance of those tests in 1986 as the highlight of their careers. To a man, they know they helped turn the direction of the Cold War.

The Submarines:

USS Hawkbill (SSN-666): Sturgeon-class attack

Nickname: The Devil Boat
Keel Laid: Vallejo CA, Mare Island Naval Shipyard
Displacement: 4363 tons submerged
Length: 292 ft
Beam: 32 ft
Draft: 29 ft
Propulsion: One S5W nuclear reactor,
Two steam turbines, one screw
Speed: 15 knots surface;
25 knots submerged
Test Depth: 1300 ft
Complement: 109 (14 officers, 95 enlisted)
Armament: Four 21-in torpedo tubes
Four Harpoon cruise missiles or up to
Eight Tomahawk land-attack cruise missiles
Commissioned: 4 February 1971
March-April '73: First submarine to operate in
Bering Strait under winter ice
March-May '86: Arctic Ops ICEX 1-86
July-Sept '98: Ops SCICEX '98
March-May'99: Ops SCICEX '99
Decommissioned: 15 March 2000
Fate: Submarine recycling program

USS Archerfish (SSN-678): Sturgeon-class attack

Keel Laid: Electric Boat/General Dynamics,
Groton, Connecticut
Displacement: 4339 tons submerged
Length: 292 ft 3 in
Beam: 31 ft 8 in
Draft: 28 ft 8 in
Installed power: 15000 shaft horsepower
Propulsion: One S5W nuclear reactor,
Two steam turbines, one screw
Speed: Over 20 knots surface;
Over 30 knots submerged
Test Depth: 1320 ft
Complement: 112 (14 officers, 98 enlisted)
Armament: Four 21-in amidship torpedo tubes;
Four Harpoon cruise missiles or up to
Eight Tomahawk land-attack cruise missiles;
Other configurations, including mines.
Commissioned: 17 December 1971
March-May'86: Arctic Ops ICEX 1-86
1988: Arctic Ops
Decommissioned: 31 March 1998
Fate: Submarine recycling program

USS Ray (SSN-653): Sturgeon-class attack

Keel Laid: Newport News Shipbuilding
Displacement: 4674 tons submerged
Length: 292 ft 3 in
Bean: 31 ft 8 in
Draft: 28 ft 8 in
Installed power: 15000 shaft horsepower
Propulsion: One S5W nuclear reactor,
Two steam turbines, one screw
Speed: 20 knots (23 mph)
Test Depth: 1300 ft

Complement: 107
Armament: Four 21-in torpedo tubes
Commissioned: 12 April 1967
March-May'86: Arctic Ops ICEX 1-86
1990: Two Arctic Ops
Decommissioned: 16 March 1993
Fate: Submarine recycling program

USSR-K240: Delta III-class, Double hull design

Keel Laid: Severodvinsk
Displacement: 18,200 tons submerged
Length: 166 m (544 ft 7 in)
Beam: 12.3 m (39 ft 6 in)
Draft: 8.8 m (29 ft)
Installed power: 60,000 shaft horsepower
Propulsion: Two nuclear reactors,
Two steam turbines, two screws
Speed: 14 knots, surface;
24 knots, submerged
Range: Unlimited, except by food supplies
Complement: 135
Armament: 16 missiles, four 533 mm (21 in)
Torpedo tubes in the bow
Commissioned: 27 November 1979
Feb-April '81: Arctic Ops and Pacific
Sept-Nov '82: Arctic Ops and Atlantic
June-Aug '84: Arctic Ops
April '86: Arctic Ops curtailed
Other Ops unknown
Fate: In reserve from 2004, probably decommissioned

References for visual and audio information on:

First Three-Submarine Rendezvous at Arctic Ice Pack:
http://www.csp.navy.mil/asl/ScrapBook/Boats/
NorthPole1986.jpg

American Submarines, see:
http://www.youtube.com/watch?v=zTohYRUt_2c&feature=related

Russian Submarines, see:
http://www.youtube.com/watch?v=zRStCCnovjM

Official U.S. Photos

ICE-X '86 Camp
Torpedo Staging---Large, Red, White and Blue Bldg.

Mining for Fresh Water: Blue Ice

Waiting for Scuba Diver

Search Diver Going Down

Lost Diver Retrieved

Helo Retrieving Torpedo-Launch Tool Shed

Sail of USS Hawkbill through Ice Pack
View from Circling Helicopter

Sail of USS Hawkbill with Secretary of Navy
and Visitors about to Board.
View from Ice Pack

Sun Down at ICE Camp '86

Movie Trailer:

ICE-X '86: Freezing the Cold War
By: L. Joseph Martini

White Screen. No Sound. In Black letters appears:

April 1986
Arctic Ice Pack

Pan Screen to:

Large blue-gray ice formations pierced with undulating shadows, in unexpectedly panoramic colors, as forty mile-an-hour sleet and snow blow diagonally across the screen. Moving forward, the camera catches the blurred image of an ice camp through the blowing snow, becoming clearer as the camera moves closer. Several Quonset huts and plywood buildings take shape, then sharpen. The camera tracks to the top of a flagpole in the center of camp. It stops on the small pennant-shaped flag with the letters "ICE-X" as it jerks in the wind. The camera tracks back down the pole, down to the ground, then through the ice into the calm underwater deep, with its semi-translucent, blue icicle formations under the ice pack. The camera continues tracking downward, revealing mammoth stalactites, hanging down to lengths of ninety feet into the Arctic Ocean.

Suddenly, a torpedo in a downward right-hand spiral crosses the screen from the left. Pinging sounds break the silence. A return ping, of slightly higher frequency, echoes back, signifying that the torpedo has acquired the body of a submarine. The camera follows the torpedo, then speeds up tracking over the body of the torpedo, passing it. Seconds later the hulk of the large dark submarine takes shape in the distance, growing larger as the camera tracks closer. The sub turns toward another group of stalactite formations in the background. The blurred image of USS.... markings on its sail are not quite legible. Then USS 666 comes clearly into view.

_____

Inside the Submarine (USS 666 Hawkbill):

Capt. Smith is standing over the helmsman when sonar man, Grahams, yells out, "Torpedo pings, Captain, approximately four thousand yards and closing."

Capt. Smith turns toward him and orders loudly, "Port heading thirty five degrees. Let's get back to that ice cave. All ahead full!

"Battle stations!"

_____

Back to the dark Arctic underwater:

The camera stops its forward motion, as the submarine moves almost out of visual range. Seconds later the torpedo comes into view, moving from right corner frame to center as it pursues the sub, visibly picking up speed. For a brief moment both the distant submarine and the torpedo in the center of the frame are simultaneously visible. Then the sub fades into the dark waters, followed seconds later by the disappearing torpedo in trail. The sounds of pinging intensify as the torpedo passes center screen, then slowly fades. The screen holds on the dark waters, neither sub nor torpedo is visible, while the pinging subsides.

_____

On the ice pack, at a launch site:

The wind howls loudly, blowing the parkas of five men gathered around a large hole in the ice. The ice camp is vaguely visible in the background. Alex Trinola and his men are dressed in dark blue, cold-weather Kevlar suits, their fur-lined hoods partially obscure shivering faces. The men struggle to steady a dual-clawed launcher loaded with a silver-gray, blunt-nosed torpedo, which hangs from the quadrupod over the hole. Two divers dressed in black, heavy-weight wet suits are in the hole. They help remove the last large ice block before they are helped out of the water that already begins to refreeze.

Trinola moves forward. He grasps the torpedo release cable in his left hand and signals with his right to lower the launcher and torpedo into the hole. Gusts of wind continue to howl around the men as they struggle to maintain their balance. The assembly is lowered into the hole through the water's surface. Alex pulls the release switch that looses the torpedo from its launcher. The torpedo jerks downward and then starts up. Its props instantly churn the water into a wake that disappears with the abating noise of the torpedo's engine. It speeds away out of view.

Alex yells into his walky-talky, "Torpedo number 14 away! Mark confirmation, Kent! Do you read?"

A scratchy voice comes through Trinola's speaker: "Affirmative, confirmation! Mark now, 11:16 and tracking torpedo 14."

A snowmobile pulls up behind the group, and a man jumps off. He moves quickly toward them. With a sheepish look on his face he apologizes, "Sorry I'm late."

Trinola, visibly annoyed, replies, "Yeah, well I know you don't have a valid excuse—just lucky nothing went wrong with that launcher of yours. Don't let this happen again, Len. We are a team up here, and every team member must be involved. The whole program may rely on anyone of us. Got that?"

Len quickly answers, "Got it, Alex."

Trinola turns his back on Len and lifts his walkie-talkie to his mouth. "Kent, any update on 13 and 14?"

Kent replies, "Number 13 just switched to secondary ping rate against the Hawkbill—closing in at thirty-two degrees, eight... [breaking up]. And number 14 is in a circular search just below where you launched it."

_____

Back onboard USS Hawkbill:

Sonar man, Grahams yells, "Ping rate switched. Hawkbill acquired! Torpedo two thousand yards and closing, Captain!"

Capt. Smith, standing over his helmsman, asks belligerently, "Damn it, where's that ice cave, Clancy?!"

Clancy at the wheel replies, "Should be two hundred yards, Captain!"

Capt. Smith commands, "Get us in there, now!"

Clancy: "Yes Sir!"

Torpedo pings are heard bouncing off the sub's hull. The camera pans around the small control room, showing crewmen with expressions of tension and fear on their faces.

_____

At the ice camp:

Camera moves from the outskirts of the camp, then through the window of a Quonset hut:

Navy divers are just stripping down to their skivvies and getting into a make-shift hot tub with two women. Suggestive music plays in the background.

Conversations between divers and two women as they splash in the water are interrupted when one of the women says, "From what I've been told our submarines aren't doing so well against those damn torpedoes."

One of the men lunges toward the woman as he says, "Here comes one now!" He mimics torpedo pings just before submerging toward her.

—————————————————————

Scene at a lunch table in the ice camp Canteen, men eating, and in conversation:

Captain Dredge talking to his military men, says, "It's not necessary for those sub skippers to know the details of these exercises! In fact, the less they know the better."

Lieut. Cameron adds, "But Sir, knowing the torpedo turn-away distance would at least give those skippers a sense of security, not to mention relief to their crew."

Distractions of loud sounds of breaking dishes in the kitchen area.

Captain Dredge replies, "No, it's not really necessary! Why, in my experience, it's just second nature to take evasive maneuvers when you hear torpedoes coming atcha. A little detail like their turn-away distance is nothing compared to knowing their sophisticated tactics. You just have to run, use countermeasures, ice formations, or whatever the hell you have to outsmart them!"

Lieut. Cameron asks, "Wait a minute, Sir...are you saying they weren't told?"

The camera pans to Trinola and his crew, who have been obviously listening in. Trinola, his coffee cup stopped mid-way to his mouth, exclaims: "What the hell!" He gets up from the table with a start, angrily moving toward Dredge's table. "WHAT did I just hear?!"

—————————————————————

A montage of quick action scenes, with voice over, and appropriate background music now appear:

Scenes:

1. An explosion of a Quonset hut, fire, men running with fire extinguishers toward it to put the fire out.

2. A polar bear circling and stalking men who are trying to recover a torpedo out of an ice hole. Trinola crouches behind a snowmobile with one of his men, Jack, who hugs his rifle aimed at the bear. The bear runs toward them, abruptly stops and rears up. Jack hesitates. The camera closes in on the fear in his face as the shot of the gun is heard.

3. The Hawkbill SSN-666 submarine breaching the Arctic ice sheet, with a helicopter circling, and men on snowmobiles approaching.

4. Underwater submarine and torpedo chase scenes.

5. Inside a Russian sub with sounds of torpedo pings. Terrified crew shouting in Russian. A final close-up of an enraged Russian sub captain shaking his fist.

Voice over:

In the spring of 1986 a top secret naval test program at the North Pole changed tactical submarine warfare forever. The story can now be told.

Based on true events, ICE-X'86 tells of a secret torpedo test team tasked to once and for all prove submarines cannot hide from torpedoes under the Arctic ice. Could this small team of torpedo experts subvert the Soviet first-strike missile threat upon the United States? Under President Ronald Reagan's "Peace through Strength" policy, U.S. submarine dominance was essential.

Alex Trinola is the torpedo team leader who must face personal struggles—mixed loyalties, self-doubt, and the Navy Brass—as well as the external obstacles of ice storms, fires, and polar bears—all on the hostile stage of the Arctic ice pack. His mission: to launch U.S. torpedoes against U.S. submarines. When a Russian submarine accidentally strays into the test range, the stakes get even higher.

When war games with submarines and torpedoes suddenly stop being games, when American engineers and seaman are tested to the breaking point, when all the Navy brass wants are results, despite the harsh weather of the Arctic ice pack, despite the exhaustion of the men and the presence of a Soviet spy in their midst, the screen explodes. Who will survive, and what nation will ultimately win in this heart-pounding competition between great enemies and greater challenges?

————————————————————————————

The screen goes black.

Main Cast of Characters:

Alex Trinola	Torpedo Team Leader
Jack Boncare	Test Engineer
Len Morini	Design Engineer
Rob O'Nerhy	Technician/Logistics
Kent Richerson	Electronics Engineer
Greg Bounds	Electronics/Strategist
Gary Tercar	Civilian Contractor
Ross Spiry	Analyst
John F. Lehman, Jr.	Secretary of the Navy
Admiral William Gooluc	CO of NOSC
Admiral James T. Watkins	Com of Naval Ops
Capt. Clifford Dredge	ICE-X Camp CO
Dr. Francos	Civilian CO of Camp
Daniels	Navy Diver
Michaelson	Navy Diver
Capt. Robert Smith	Capt. of USS Hawkbill
Lt. Com. Jonathan Maple	CO of USS Hawkbill
Grahams	Sonar man on Hawkbill
Clancy	Helmsman on Hawkbill
Capt. Koresh	Capt. of USS Archerfish
Lt. Com. Reigle	CO of USS Archerfish
"Ears"	Sonar man/ Archerfish
Capt. Leonid Glamouri	Capt. of USSR-K240
Lieut. Mishky	CO of USSR-K240